DEADLY CATCH

SAWYER BLACK

STERLING & STONE

DEADLY CATCH

Chapter One

When Mark Adler cut the engine to let the boat drift into a turn that lifted it over the swell of his own wake, the woman in the seat next to him squeaked in dismay and lunged for the plastic handles in front of her. He covered his smile by putting his sunglasses on before standing up from behind the wheel on legs trained to walk on churning seas.

He winced at the pain that shot up from his right shin — the old injury that had sent him into retirement from the Navy — but it didn't dampen his spirit. He couldn't help that his smile spread into a grin as he passed her muttered curses on his way to help her husband with the fishing pole. Another wave slapped at the side of the boat, dropping them into its trough as it passed.

"Jesus Christ," she spat. "You said it was calm out here."

As soon as he had first seen her, Mark knew he would forget her name. He was sure he would remember her attitude, though. He grinned at her over his shoulder. "It *is* calm."

The muscles in her toned shoulders tightened as she held on. Maybe forty years old, she was still a good twenty-five years younger than her man. Obvious care went into her skin and body, but it looked like most of the benefit came from money. One quick look at her breasts straining the fabric of her yellow bikini top told him a story. The size of the diamond on her ring was another chapter. The clueless smile on her husband's face finished it, and the amount of money Mark had been paid for the trip was the epilogue.

Her husband, Harold Perlmutter, tightened the string that held his wide-brimmed straw hat on his head. His tight Lycra shirt stretched over his protruding belly under a chest so thin, Mark wondered how he had the breath to speak.

"Calm down, Nancy," Harold said.

Nancy. *That* was her name.

She turned in her seat and pointed at her husband's face. "Don't tell me to calm down, *Harold*."

One more big wave was coming, so Mark braced against the sidewall with his good knee and grabbed Harold's bony shoulder. A rocking rise followed by a stomach-churning drop, and Nancy slid off the edge of her cushion to land on her ass with a splat.

Instead of the anger he expected, Nancy responded by throwing her head back in a laugh. The first sound she had made that didn't set Mark's teeth on edge.

He pushed Harold to stay put as he rushed to help Nancy up, but she waved him away, her face flush with mirth and embarrassment.

She folded her legs under her and stood with one smooth motion. Mark winced at the thought of doing that to his bad knee.

Nancy's laugh diminished as the waves passed and the boat settled.

"Are you okay, dear?" Harold asked.

A rueful shake of her head as she passed by the controls to climb to the foredeck. "I'm fine, Harold. I guess I just needed to *calm down*."

Mark moved aft past Harold to the anchor. As he threw it over and guided the line, he looked up at the older man. "Is she seriously alright?"

Harold grabbed the rail to steady himself. He slid his hat back to expose his balding head, wisps of white hair fluttering in the warm breeze. The smear of zinc oxide on his nose glowed in the sun. "Oh, yes. Sometimes she just needs to be steered toward fun."

"I heard that!" Nancy said.

"Of course you did, dear."

Mark turned to look back at her. Lithe and tan, she relaxed onto a towel that matched her swimsuit. She tilted her hat over her face and laid her arms along her side. A movement that struck Mark as elegant.

When he found Harold watching him with a smile, he almost blushed. He shrugged before moving to grab the bait pail.

"She's great," he said, and he surprised himself by meaning it.

Harold sighed as he jammed his hat back down and tightened the drawstring. "Yes, she is. And did you know, she's fifty?"

"Watch it!" Nancy shouted.

Harold's eyes twinkled. "We've been married for twenty-one years. Were a secret couple for years before that. And in all that time, no matter how she may have complained, when I looked back, I always found her there."

Mark wanted to look away. Harold must have picked up on his initial dislike of Nancy.

He grabbed a pole and freed the hook as an excuse to break eye contact.

"I'm sixty-seven," Harold continued.

Only seventeen years older than her? Mark froze with incredulity to stare back at the old man.

Harold chuckled. "I wonder if you will look as good after fighting off three different types of cancer."

"I'm sorry."

"Don't be. I'm not going to beat the fourth one. That's why I'm here. I'm dying, Mr. Adler. My wife is having more difficulty coming to terms with it than I am. She is often cross with me and others, wanting me to *recline* as I decline—"

Nancy snorted laughter.

"But I would rather spend my final moments having an adventure. That's why I'm paying your daily rate plus a thousand dollars."

Mark looked at Nancy. With one knee up, she suddenly looked regal. Why had he thought she was such a bitch before?

He set the pole Harold would be using on the rest and bent to trim the squid into bait-sized chunks.

"But why me?" Mark asked. "There were other charters available."

"Because the others only guaranteed me a good time. *You* said you guaranteed I would catch a fish. Then you guaranteed we would find a lobster. Then you said you would show me how to cook it. Then you said you had green beans in your houseboat that you had canned fresh this season from your sister's garden in Michigan, and that we were welcome to them. Mr. Adler—"

"Call me Mark, please."

4

Harold tipped a small salute at the edge of his floppy bill. "Mark, you offered more of yourself to us than the others, and that was before a discussion of price. Where the others were ogling, you were admiring. And where the others looked at me with knowing contempt, you looked at me with sympathy."

Mark burned with embarrassment. He didn't think Harold's assessment of him was accurate ... or warranted. Sure, he had offered all that, but it was just what he did for everybody. And as far as not looking at his wife? Mark had no longer thought Nancy was that attractive after hearing her complain all the way from the dock to the shallow waters that he liked to fish, east of Sediment Key. After her musical laughter, though, he could stand to get another eyeful.

He had to change the subject.

"Anybody want a drink?" he asked.

Nancy sat up like a meerkat investigating a distant sound. She clapped her hands in front of her chest. "Ooh, yes."

Mark had a bulk recipe for margaritas. A gallon batch at a time with a homemade orange liqueur topper. They were a big hit back at camp, where all the other veterans gathered every evening to talk about the glory days. He pointed at the beige Yeti cooler behind the control station.

"In that cooler are some strong margaritas and ice. Dixie cups in a bag next to it."

She slid off her towel to open the lid. "I thought this was for fish."

"Would you mind, dear?" Harold asked.

She looked up at Harold over the top of her glasses. "Women's work, is it?"

"Yes," Harold stated with a satisfied smile.

Mark sputtered an apology, but Nancy laughed again.

If it wasn't her body, it was that sound that surely had made Harold fall in love with her.

"I'm kidding," she said. "Your hands are already fishy."

And with that, it turned into an easy day. Like three old friends getting to know each other after a long time apart.

Harold recounted his breathless joy at catching his first fish. "I went with my brother ages ago when I was a boy," he said. "Down the levee by the Chesterton River. There, he gave me a pole and a plug of Steiner Wintergreen Tobacco. I threw up all over the clay bank and swore to everybody that I absolutely hated fishing."

The old man stood steady at the rail in spite of Nancy feeding him drink after drink. "Nothing wrong with my liver. I beat *that* cancer last spring. No, this time it's in my lungs."

Mark realized the redness on Harold's nose under the zinc oxide wasn't an old sunburn, but the broken blood vessels of alcohol abuse. He'd seen it in many of his friends. Even the shadow of it in his own reflection sometimes.

After catching a cooler full of grunts — Nancy had screamed in laughter when she heard them grunting and squealing like pigs in the bottom of the bucket — Mark took them to a few shallow wrecks where he knew lobsters liked to hide. An easy dive with a tickle stick — a two-foot rod of aluminum with a small crook on the end — and his lobster glove, and soon there were eight of them in the other cooler.

Harold sputtered in surprise when Mark had delivered the first one into his hands. He laughed, bent over to cough, then sat down to rest with a beaming grin and wide eyes.

Nancy took gentle care of her husband, making sure he was fine with quiet questions and knowing looks, then comforting him with a soft touch of assurance in the center of his back.

The small restroom below deck got a workout, and the bed nestled at the bow finally got somebody other than a drunk Mark when Harold eased into it after calling it a day. The margaritas were all gone, and they had gone through every snack Mark had brought — including a charcuterie tray he had gotten at Aldi.

With the sun kissing the tops of the mangrove trees, Mark pulled the anchor and turned to find Nancy standing next to the controls, watching him.

"I'm sorry," he blurted.

"Why?"

"I didn't like you at first."

"*That's* why you're sorry?"

"Well, that and … Harold. I obviously don't know what he was like before, but he seems like a guy I might have enjoyed being around. It sucks that he's … you know."

"I do." Her eyes glittered with tears as she ducked down the stairs to sit on the bed next to Harold's hip. She took his hand in hers, and Mark swallowed the burn of unwanted emotion in his throat.

He took it nice and slow on the way back, and by the time the boat scraped against the rubber bumpers on the dock, Harold was back on his feet, ready for more.

Nancy went into the dock offices to buy a few beers and some kind of flavored vodka seltzer with the picture of a pink wolf on the can, while Mark showed Harold how to clean and fillet the fish. The old man jumped in with fascination, and when they finished, they had several pounds of fish ready to cook, and eight deveined lobster tails. The setting sun glittered in Harold's wide, glassy eyes as Nancy cracked open a third beer for him.

"I can't thank you enough for today," Harold said.

Mark bent to lift the cooler up to the counter to keep them from seeing his face turn red. "It was my pleasure. You got something we can put all this fish in?"

"Oh no," Harold said. "You keep it. I've eaten fish before, but I've never *caught* one. I wanted the experience, and you gave it to me."

Mark set the cooler back down. "I can't take all this."

"You said you have fish fries all the time. Have another one. On me."

Harold stepped forward and grabbed Mark's shoulder. Before he could stop him, he leaned in and kissed Mark on the lips before pulling him into an awkward embrace. "Thank you. So much."

Harold spun away and walked toward the gravel parking lot. He looked at the upper crescent of the setting sun and whistled a familiar tune Mark couldn't quite identify.

Nancy stepped in front of him. Mark held his arms open. "You gonna kiss me, too?"

Her grin flashed as she nodded her head, but tears spilled down her cheeks. She pulled him into a tender kiss before putting her head on his chest.

"He only has a few weeks left," she whispered. "Thank you for this memory of him being so ... *happy*."

Mark didn't understand what she meant. He had just done what he would normally do. He was still trying to puzzle it out when she stepped back and wiped her eyes. The breeze had cooled, and in her yellow bikini, she had nothing but her hat and bag to block it. The fading light burned an aura around her as she walked away to meet Harold at the dark SUV they had arrived in. They both waved before getting in, and Harold laid his head back against the passenger seat headrest.

Mark waved back, and the parking lot lights came on with an orange swell. He knew he'd remember them forever now. They were people he didn't even really know, but if never seeing a stranger again was better than missing somebody he loved, why did seeing their taillights fade into the night hurt so much?

Mark pulled his phone out to call Longjohn Hastings, an old Navy friend who used to be the Sediment Key Harbor Master.

"Hey, hey." The voice was distorted, so Mark knew Longjohn was talking through his ancient Bluetooth headset.

"You wanna get the fryer ready? Maybe a bottle of tequila too?"

"You bet."

Longjohn hung up without saying goodbye. He must have been playing Call of Duty with his grandson.

It would only take ten minutes for Mark to get the boat on the trailer, and another ten to get to the campsite. Midnight should see him full and buzzed and ready to sleep without nightmares.

It wasn't until he got behind the wheel of his Jeep that he realized Harold had never paid him.

For some reason, it made him like the man even more.

Chapter Two

Jennifer St. James settled back into the leather seat as the armored limo rolled into Islamorada, leaving the view of the ocean outside her window behind. She tugged the hem of her short white skirt toward her knees, but Reg's hand fell on hers, making the fabric snap back up, exposing the bottom of the tattoo swirling around the outside of her thigh.

Her mother sat across from her. Janet — never Mother or Mom — arched an eyebrow when her gaze flickered down to the scrolling thorns that made up the St. James Protection logo on Jennifer's skin, the company Jennifer owned with her parents.

Jennifer knew she had a majority share only to clean up their taxes. Like her mother, she wasn't allowed any real decision making. No purpose for being there other than to sell an image. Just like her father's beard.

He sat across from Jennifer with his hand on Janet's thigh, a bald beast of a man with a long wild beard that Janet had convinced him to grow, saying it made him look mean. Just for show, like her.

Like Jennifer.

He wore soft faded jeans and a white button-up shirt with the sleeves rolled up to reveal his thick forearms. He maintained his impressive physique with a brutal workout regimen supplemented by a nauseating amount of red meat and steroids. He had convinced Reg to start taking them too, and even though Reg wasn't as disciplined as her father, he had made substantial gains.

The muscles in Reg's shoulders and neck seemed to be growing as fast as his testicles were shrinking, and his sex drive was through the roof. Maybe if he wasn't having so much trouble getting an erection, he might be a little more forgiving.

But as soon as the bitterness of the thought entered Jennifer's mind, Reg squeezed her fingers. Warm and reassuring, it made her look up at him and smile. He smiled back. Wide and playful, it crinkled his eyes at the corners and reminded her of why she fell for him two years ago.

Her father, Don — never Father or Dad, though he let Reg call him Pops — slapped Janet's thigh like he'd suddenly remembered something. The sharp crack sounded painful, but Janet seemed to barely notice. Jennifer had seen Don do it a thousand times.

He pointed at Reg. "Did you set up the meeting with that trainer? The one with the kill houses in Carlin Beach?"

Jennifer looked over to meet Janet's gaze. Her mother grabbed Don's hand and put it back on her thigh, right where the impact had been.

"Oh yeah," Reg said. "Brad Chester."

"Charter," Jennifer corrected.

Reg's reassuring grip became a crushing pincer. She clenched her jaw to keep from crying out as he bore down.

"That's right," he said. She could hear the reproach in

his voice, though she doubted her parents knew it was there.

He let her go to point at the ceiling, a gesture he used as acknowledgement. "*Charter*. Thanks, babe."

Jennifer knew the customer list back to front. She could recognize them by the sound of their voices over the phone. Reg was still learning the business; he'd been hired for his looks and contacts more than his knowledge about private security.

He brought with him a key that opened doors, and a team of veterans he had served with. A military man her parents had melted for.

She couldn't blame them, though. *She* had melted for him, too.

St. James Protection specialized in private security for the extremely wealthy. The bigger the client, the bigger the guns. They could be loud and visible or quiet and barely discernible from the surrounding shadows.

The company handled escorts through Mexico and South America that might or might not be funded by drugs, celebrities filming or interviewing in foreign countries, South African cash transfers by armored truck, and more. Their broad and extensive history had made the St. James family nearly a hundred million dollars.

The next step was government funding. Train and place private security agents in schools to respond to active shooters, and that grant money would roll in. Reg seemed to know the people to talk to for the specific training required. Jennifer could see St. James Protection in schools all across America … and it sickened her.

She had learned the business from her father. Trained in mixed martial arts and tactical weapons handling to make him proud. She worked out and moisturized and shaved and plucked for her mother. The perfect application of bronzer, and where to dab the fragrance.

She wore the short skirt for Reg. G-strings, when he let her wear panties at all. For months, the insides of her thighs would ache from keeping her knees pressed together for fear that her mother would catch a glimpse from across the limo.

When she first realized he didn't love her, and probably never had, she had breathed a silent sigh of relief. She wasn't sure *what* he loved. Her parents, for sure. Money and power. His friends. Cruelty.

She thought about the men following in the matching SUV, a show of force for anybody wanting to know what St. James was all about. Another delicious farce suggested by Reg and lapped up by her adoring parents.

She often talked to herself in the mirror. Gave her reflection a high five. "You can do it. You're more than what people expect of you. You're smart and pretty and blah blah blah."

The only thing keeping her going was habit. The routine of guilt and fear.

"We can send Jennifer," Reg said.

Jennifer straightened like she had been poked in the ribs. "Huh?"

"My goodness," Janet said. "Where is your head at?"

Jennifer knew dwelling on an apology would just piss them all off.

"Sorry, I was thinking about a meeting I have to take next week."

"What meeting?" Reg demanded.

Don grinned. "That's work stuff. Let's put our phones down and be a family, right?"

Jennifer grinned back. Not once had he ever laid a

finger on her in anger, but whenever his face sagged in disappointment, she felt buried under uncontrollable shame. Janet had always been the one to dole out punishment.

"You're right. What did I miss?"

Reg took her hand again, but this time he didn't crush it. "I was saying we could send you to the training course in Carlin. You would be amazing."

Even that small approval made her warm with pride, followed by a wash of cold disgust with herself for needing it.

"You know," Reg said. "Like that Geico commercial."

Don laughed. A giggle much higher than his gruff speaking voice. "Wasn't that cavemen?"

"Same difference."

Jennifer pulled her hand free of Reg's grasp. "Cavemen and girls aren't the same thing."

"I don't get it," Janet said.

Don turned to her with a long-suffering smile. "He's saying have Jennifer do the course to prove it's so easy, even a girl can do it."

"But girls *can't* do it," Janet said.

Jennifer drew herself up straight. "Hey."

"That's not what I mean. You're just so good, you don't represent *girls*."

"Thank you, I guess?"

"But that's my point," Reg said. "Somebody outside looking in won't know how good she is until she does it."

Don scratched his ear in confusion. "I don't know. You've been with us long enough to know she has a reputation within the community. She's made the company proud."

Reg pointed at the ceiling. "You're right. Then maybe we should do it to show how badass St. James Protection is."

Don nodded, his face slack in thought. "I like that." He brightened as he looked up at Jennifer. "How about it, kitten?"

The thought of undergoing active shooter training turned her stomach. The counterterrorism training she had participated in last year had left her unable to sleep from stress and anxiety. Her hair had come out in thin clumps until the training was over. Maintaining the face of a robot as men screamed in her ear to kill kill *kill*!

She smiled and snuggled up to Reg. "It sounds like fun, but I thought we weren't talking about work stuff."

Don shrugged with a *you got me* smile. "My bad."

Janet leaned to the side to grab her purse. She started the last-minute makeup touch-ups before they pulled into the restaurant. Jennifer waited a few moments before following suit, to make it look like she *wasn't* following. A quick once-over to satisfy anybody who might be watching — because she had learned there was *always* somebody watching.

They were headed to some actor's house after dinner. Carter Hyatt from *These Hot Streets*. She'd never heard of it before Reg had made her get a subscription to Starz as "research." She could barely get through the first episode.

It was a party nobody seemed to want to go to except Reg. He said it would be good networking.

Reg rolled his cuffs up to match Don. Jennifer wondered if he meant to do it or if it was a habit now. "You still going out on the yacht tomorrow?"

Don grimaced. "It's not a yacht."

Janet patted his leg. "Yes it is, honey."

Reg spread his hands in a *what are you gonna do?* shrug.

"Okay, fine," Don said. "Yes, we're taking it out. Lobster in Key West, then up the Atlantic for lobster in

Maine. We're stopping for a few days at the house in Key Largo, though. I got a dentist thing."

"You'll be back in time for the quarterly meeting?" Reg asked.

"Maybe. There's always Zoom, you know."

"Yeah, but it's not the same."

"Why the interest in having us there in person?" Don's smile told Jennifer he knew exactly why Reg wanted him there. "Something you're not telling me?"

Reg's laugh sounded forced. "You know there's no other man for me than you."

Jennifer glanced at Janet, both of them held hostage in this weird homoerotic game men often played.

"We were meant for each other, that's true," Don said.

Reg scooted to the edge of the seat and leaned forward. "I just … I think I've proven myself. I'm opening doors for St. James Protection. I'm landing clients."

Jennifer knew those clients had been hers long before he claimed them, but nobody was willing to set him straight.

"That's true," Don said.

Jennifer could tell Reg thought he was going to get what he wanted. "Right, and you trust me with your daughter. So, how about you trust me with a little bit more. Trust me with your *other* baby."

Don leaned back with a sigh. "Restructuring the company to give you an ownership share is just not practical at this point. I know you think it will make you even more a part of this family than you already are, but Janet and I have to disagree. You couldn't be any more our son than you are now. Besides, you have Jennifer's shares, if something were to happen to her."

"God forbid," Janet said.

Reg leaned back, a mirror image to Don. "But then we

wouldn't have *her*. What good would it be if she fell off the boat and drowned tomorrow? Sure, I'd get her share, but then—"

Janet slapped her purse onto the seat next to her. "Can we please not talk about my daughter being dead?"

The specificity of his description of how she might die made Jennifer tense in alarm. While her parents were traveling on their yacht, Reg had planned for her to stay in Key West with him. A fishing trip on a boat run by a retired Navy officer that one of his men had recommended. The twitch under Reg's eye and the clenching of his jaw made her pull away from him. Then he smiled, and the tension bled away.

Reg pointed at the ceiling. "You're right. I'm so sorry, Janet. I just … I just want to make you proud."

"We *are* proud, so don't be so morbid. You're the best thing to happen to Jennifer."

She wanted to jump up and scream, "Nothing just *happens* to me! I'm not some passive decoration on a shelf waiting for somebody to admire me!"

Instead, she took Reg's hand. Smiled at her father. Put herself on the very shelf that would show her off as an achievement, as if the men in her life had earned her beauty and ability through any work of their own.

The limos parked in the reserved section of the lot with a view of the setting sun sparkling off the beach. Reg and Don got out first. Jennifer and her mother followed, both of them smoothing hair and skirts and staying a half-step behind.

Jennifer wanted to jump off the shelf. To throw herself into the air to escape the scrutiny and judgment she felt. Not from strangers, but from the members of her own family.

But she was afraid of the fall. As strong as she pretended to be, she knew she would shatter.

Chapter Three

Mark stood over the heat of the fryer. He pulled the last strainer of fish out of the oil as he tipped his can up to his lips to catch the last few drops of beer. Some German lager a retired Marine sniper had brought.

Somebody else had given Mark a cranberry IPA that had taken two years off of his life with just the first sip.

He waved a mosquito away from his face. Staying close to Longjohn's cigar smoke usually kept them at bay, but the spitting oil seemed to attract them. At least the base had mowed all the sites yesterday, so the no-see-ums weren't too bad.

A screened tent they had set up behind him kept the food safe from bugs and curious dogs. Like most nights, his simple fish fry had turned into an impromptu potluck. Many old faces he recognized from previous weeks, and plenty of new people rotating in to keep things feeling fresh.

But it never seemed entirely new. As he reached for a fresh beer, Mark had to admit that he was getting tired. He tried to make a mental list of how he was adding anything truly meaningful to the world. A very *short* list.

Catching and cooking fish was how he pretended to contribute, but it was really so he could avoid the crowds. Always at sea with strangers. Then, huddling in the corner with his pot so he could use the duty of frying the fish as an excuse to keep from having to engage with anyone.

It *looked* like he was a part of the lives of those around him, but it really kept him away. A distance just out of reach to keep him safe from their sympathy, but just close enough to look like he wasn't actively avoiding them.

One of the new guys was a young infantryman staying on base while he and his new wife trolled Duval Street for the week leading up to a series of classic rock concerts at the waterfront amphitheater. Dwayne and Tracy Tate. She was small and blonde. He was shaved bald. Thick neck and sagging love handles, like he had once been obese. He was somebody's nephew, but Mark was too drunk to remember who.

Dwayne carried a bottle of Crown Royal everywhere he went while looking over his shoulder to make sure Tracy was right behind him. She rarely looked up from her feet, and Mark wasn't sure if he had seen her eat anything.

Dwayne approached to step through the blowing steam to stick his hand out in greeting. "You're the one they say we have to thank for the fish," he said through a grin under a glassy-eyed stare.

Tracy must not have been paying attention. She collided with Dwayne's back, and Canadian whiskey slopped out of the open bottle.

Dwayne's friendly smile became a snarl as he spun to grab Tracy's upper arm. Her eyes widened in shock, but when Dwayne's fingers sunk in, she grunted in pain, lifting up on her tiptoes as Dwayne pulled her close.

"Jesus, can you just watch where you're going for one fucking minute?"

"I'm sorry," she gasped.

Mark looked to either side to see if anybody had noticed, but nobody stood near him at the rear of Longjohn's RV where they had set his table up. He dropped his strainer with a sigh and reached for Dwayne's shoulder. "Come on, man."

Dwayne released Tracy and shrugged Mark's hand off his shoulder. "Come on, what?"

"Don't do that shit here. In fact, I'd prefer you didn't do it *anywhere*."

Tracy rubbed the red dimples sunk into the skin of her arm. Tears glistened on her cheeks as she smiled. "It was my fault, really."

There was a scream behind her eyes.

"Do what?" Dwayne said to Mark.

Mark pointed at Tracy's arm. "Grabbing her like that. She didn't do anything."

Tracy held her hands up like she was being robbed. "No, please. I wasn't watching where I was going." The pain on her face became panic.

Dwayne set his bottle down and took a bouncing step toward Mark. "It's none of your business, bro."

"You're in fucking public, dipshit. It's everybody's business."

Longjohn stepped around the corner with an empty paper plate. Johnnie *Longjohn* Hastings was a lumbering bear in basketball shorts and a billowing tank top. His long hair and beard still had black in it, but it was mostly white, yellowing around his mouth from the nicotine of his two-pack-a-day habit.

He wore compression socks like Mark, but where Mark wore them because of the injury, Longjohn wore them because of diabetic neuropathy. Size fifteen Crocs. "And you're on my site standing next to my rig," he said.

Dwayne spun around and tipped his head back to look up at Longjohn's face. "And who the fuck are you?"

Longjohn ignored him to look from Mark to Tracy. He touched her shoulder. "Are you okay, girl?"

Dwayne jumped forward to swipe at Longjohn's hand. "Get your hands off—"

Mark lunged to grab Dwayne's wrist. Dwayne twisted away, but Mark held fast as he easily dropped under Dwayne's drunken punch.

Their momentum combined to give Mark leverage. He continued his spin to bring Dwayne's hand behind his back, jerking up to put enough stress on his shoulder to bring Dwayne up on his toes.

"Get the fuck off me!" Dwayne shouted.

Mark pushed Dwayne into the corner of Longjohn's RV. He looked back to see Tracy rocking from her toes to her heels like she was unable to decide to help Dwayne or not. Or maybe she wanted to help Mark.

Longjohn stood behind her with a smile and a sad shake of his head. "Let him go, Mark."

Mark leaned back to put more pressure on Dwayne's arm. "If I let you go … if I get the fuck off you, will you settle down?"

"Fuck you."

People from the fish fry turned to watch. Now Mark was no longer hidden.

Longjohn stepped in front of Tracy. "Let him go, I said."

Mark let go and hopped back with his hands held up in defense, but Dwayne just turned with a growl to rub his shoulder. He reached out for his wife. "Come on, Tracy. This is bullshit."

"You're right," Longjohn said. "Putting your hands on a woman *is* bullshit."

"What do you know, old man?"

"I know you have some anger in you, son. I can see it because I've had it in *me*."

Dwayne snapped his fingers. "Let's fucking go."

Longjohn shook his head and stepped to the side to block Tracy from going to her husband. "Not yet. See, I'm afraid you'll get back to your site, and take your anger out on her."

"He won't," she said.

Dwayne shook his head like he disagreed with her, but he said, "I won't."

Mark didn't believe either of them.

Longjohn tipped his head toward Mark. "I don't want you starting anything with that man, because you wouldn't be able to finish it."

"Whatever." A sullen whisper.

"But me? I'm the nicest guy in the world. So, I'm gonna let you take it out on me." Longjohn put his hands behind his back and leaned forward to stick his chin out. "So, go ahead. Take your best shot. But before you do, know that if you leave me standing, unlike Tracy here, I'll hit back. But if you manage — by some *miracle* — to put me down, you'll have to deal with Mark, and he is not nearly as nice as I am."

Longjohn's eyes no longer smiled. They were cold and dead, like pellets of glass flickering with reflected firelight.

"Whatever," Dwayne repeated. "Let's go, Trace."

"She can stay," Longjohn said.

Pam Lawes, a retired Air Force pilot walked around Longjohn to stand next to Tracy. Her white braid fell across her shoulder like it belonged to a Disney princess. "That might be best," she said.

Tracy seemed uncertain, until Pam put her arm across her shoulder. Tracy closed her eyes and collapsed into the older woman, crying in a sudden release that made Mark want to tear Dwayne's head off.

Longjohn took another step toward Dwayne. "How about it?"

Dwayne sagged in defeat. "Man, I'm drunk."

Longjohn straightened with disgust. "If that excuse was worth a shit, we'd all be saints. Go home."

"What about Tracy?"

"She'll decide or she won't, but I know you and I aren't going to do it for her."

Dwayne nodded like it was the most reasonable thing he had ever heard. He turned with a wave and shuffled past the gathering crowd.

Pam led Tracy away with a comforting murmur in her ear.

"Hey, hey!" Longjohn shouted. He threw his arm over Mark's shoulder. "You eat yet?"

Mark shook his head as he watched Pam and Tracy disappear into a group of women that swirled around them like birds. "I was about to."

"Well, hurry up, I wanna open that tequila."

Mark closed the valve on the propane and turned to follow Longjohn to the tent, but he paused when he saw the Crown Royal Dwayne had left behind. He picked it up with a shrug and took a drink before carrying the fish to the tent.

Chapter Four

Jennifer saw Reg looking at her over the lip of his bourbon glass. She knew he only drank it because Don did. The way the skin tightened under his eyes whenever he swallowed a sip told her he didn't like it.

His gaze flickered away like he had been caught staring at a stranger.

She swallowed the last of her wine and put the empty glass on a marble table under a gold-framed mirror. The style of Carter Hyatt's house was subdued neo-luxury. The kind of decorating done by someone who had only had pictures of interior design described to them over the phone. Sterile stones and metals covered in thick textiles to make it looked lived in. A fuzzy blanket. Pillow piles covering the sleek sofa.

It felt like a movie set.

She had hardly eaten at the restaurant. A small salmon salad while her mother watched. Jennifer needed more protein than that, but it was difficult choking it down when she was being judged. Janet seemed not to mind the two raspberry sours Jennifer had put down at the bar, though. Especially since she was ahead by two glasses of her own.

When they left the restaurant for the after party, the back of the limo smelled like a distillery. Every conversation they had lately seemed to be fueled by alcohol. Especially the professional ones.

Jennifer didn't know how to make small talk. She usually smiled as prettily as she could before excusing herself. Or she sat in Reg's shadow and pretended to listen. Thankfully, the party was a chaotic rave of punishingly loud music in a dimly lit Florida mansion. There wasn't much talking.

Don and Janet danced on the patio next to the pool. They looked like they belonged with the other guests. People Reg called "Hollywood players." Some of them looked like high school runaways. Others were desperately clinging to youth. Many of them were gifted with perfect skin and hair and bodies as they skated through life on a whim.

All of them were fake.

She glanced at herself in the mirror over her empty wine glass. She fit right in.

A woman calling herself Carter's spiritual advisor had met them at the door. She had no idea who they were, but she assumed they were supposed to be there. The way she kissed the air in front of Jennifer's lips in greeting proved it was all an act. She told them "Cart" would find them, and to make themselves at home.

"The bathrooms are down the grass hallway," she'd cried with a brilliant grin. Like she had told them the name of her lord and savior. She pointed the way into the kitchen as she twirled away to rush back into the party. The lights from the DJ's table shone through her sheer dress. She wasn't wearing underwear.

Jennifer pulled the hem of her skirt down before following Reg inside.

The security team spread out into the front yard behind them. Jennifer rolled her eyes at the absurd show, but Reg nodded in enthusiastic approval. Don had slapped him on the shoulder with a beaming smile of pride.

Jennifer tore her gaze from her reflection. Reg had turned to talk to an older man in a neat suit, so she took her chance to get away for a moment alone.

Down a white hallway into a kitchen built to look like an outdoor café. Uniformed staff bustled at the huge island preparing more food for the party. Behind them was a wall of windows with a view of the sparling ocean a few hundred yards past a row of elephant ears that shielded the pool. Half-naked girls walking on tiptoe. The multi-colored glitter of drinks swirling in expensive glasses.

How had she let herself get caught up in all this? Why didn't she have the guts to push past the pretend?

She turned to thread through a group wandering by on their way to sit at a long table with a scattering of board games across it.

Two wide hallways opened off the opposite side of the kitchen. Marble and stucco to the left. A dark wood floor and walls covered in grass on the right. She followed the spiritual partner's directions to the restroom.

After a bend, she found two doors separated by a water fountain that looked like a urinal. Each door had a stylized sign above it. BOYS OR/AND GIRLS. A crayon couple entwined as if dancing.

What kind of house had two bathrooms in it just for party guests?

She picked the closest one. Like the restroom at a chain restaurant, it opened into a tiled room. A long sink with three basins. Four stainless steel stalls. One Roman shower.

The middle stall flushed, and she shied away from the echo to the first stall. The middle door banged open, and a man in a cream-colored linen suit staggered out. He veered toward her to stop in front of her. He threw his hand up as if to brace against the metal, but it also blocked her into the corner.

His eyes were like glistening pools. His breath was booze and weed. "You're a pretty little thing," he said. "How about you be pretty for *me*?"

Her initial stab of fear fell into disgust. "That's the best you have?"

His brow furrowed like he was working through some difficult math. "What do you mean?"

"You just tell me I'm pretty, and I'm supposed to what? Give you my panties?"

He smiled. "If it's that easy, yeah." He reached up to touch the strands of hair that had pulled out of her ponytail, but she ducked under his hand and stepped to his outside foot. She pushed his elbow and shoulder into his rotation, and he slammed into the wall.

His knees buckled, but he kept on his feet. She stepped back and relaxed her balled fist. "Wash your fucking hands."

She stalked to the end stall and slammed the door behind her, throwing the bolt. She waited until she heard the water at the sink flow as the creep took her advice to heart. She had no doubt she could take a drunk douchebag with little problem, but she shouldn't have been in the situation in the first place.

This was how relationships and businesses ended.

The water stopped to be replaced by the scream of a hand dryer. Saving the environment, one eardrum at a time.

Don would have laughed at the joke, but he would

have been pissed to find his little Tinkerbell caught by an asshole in the bathroom. She wasn't sure what Reg would do. Or what either would do if some asshole actually attacked her. She knew Don would have gone insane. Partly because he wanted to protect his little girl, but mostly because he protected what was *his*.

She finished with a dab of toilet paper — something her mother called *cleaning the ladybug*. The hand dryer finally shut off, and she stepped out to take her own advice, only the creep was still there.

He stood in the alcove leading to the door.

The fear that had turned into disgust became excitement. An expectant vibration that went through her like an evening shiver. The air freshener above the mirrors spritzed into the silence. The mist brought lavender and peppermint to her nose.

"What are you doing?" she asked.

He blinked as he stepped forward. "I don't know."

"What, did I make you angry?"

He looked up at the ceiling before nodding. "Yeah."

"Are you drunk?"

"Yeah."

She sighed, and her excitement faded back into disgust. "What do you want? Is this some dominant rape fantasy come true for you?"

He jerked back as if she had slapped him. "What? No! Jesus, what's wrong with you?"

She had left her small purse in the car. That meant her gun was in there, too. All she had were her hands and her training. "You're the one who cornered a woman in the restroom, Lester."

"My name's not—"

"I don't give a shit." Jennifer took two big steps to put herself right under his chin. He stood his ground, but he drew his head back like a kid trying not to eat that first bite of peas. She jabbed her finger into his chest. "You don't fucking *do* that. And if you want your ass kicked, keep it up."

He swallowed and looked down the front of her top with an incredulous sneer. "Who? *You?*"

She feigned a kick to his balls to make brushing contact with her knee against his thigh. His instincts made him throw his hips back and thrust both hands out in front of him.

Jennifer grabbed his left wrist and pivoted under it to internally rotate his shoulder, forcing him into a spin to keep it in its socket. She brought the hand up behind him and stomped on the back of his knee. He dropped down with a groan, and she pushed against the back of his head to press his cheek into the wall.

The door swung open, and two bubbly blondes bounced in. The first one squealed in dismay, but the second pushed her into the bathroom like a woman holding a man against the wall was the most natural thing in the world.

"Get him, girl!" she cried.

Shame burned up Jennifer's spine. Her face heated, and the bathroom became a beige blur as tears welled in her eyes. She had *wanted* to hurt him.

She leaned in to put her mouth next to the creep's ear. "They will fuck you up if they see you near me, but it's nothing compared to what they're doing to me."

"The hell's wrong with you, lady?"

Jennifer stepped back and wiped her eyes. "I don't know."

She rushed back into the grass hallway and was halfway through the kitchen before she realized she hadn't washed her hands.

Chapter Five

If Mark went to bed sober, the nightmares were always sharp and detailed. Like a perfectly replayed memory. He would wake up sweating and breathless. Go to the bathroom for some ibuprofen and a glass of water, then back to bed for the nightmares to start again.

He'd tried different antidepressants, taking weeks to give each one a chance to work while cataloging the side effects.

Insomnia. Sleeping *too* much. On some, his dick stopped working. On others, it worked just fine, but he couldn't get off. Or he lost interest in sex altogether. GI problems. Sun sensitivity. Manic thoughts of motion where he had to be moving all the time, doing *something* or he felt like he would *explode*.

Most of them interacted with his pain meds, especially the ones he took for nerve pain.

After a year and a half cycling through the options, he decided to try medicating with the only substance that had ever worked to subdue the guilt with the least amount of obvious side effects.

Alcohol.

With a good buzz, he went to sleep as soon as his head hit the pillow. Slept for a few hours like a dead man before waking up, unable to fall back to sleep. But there were no nightmares. A hard workout in the morning, followed by two miles as fast as his bum leg could carry him, and he was good for the day. Unless he got drunk, which happened more often than he wanted.

If he went to bed drunk, he fell asleep and stayed asleep, but the nightmares found him. Not the hazy version of reality he was used to, but fractured and abstract scenes of sound and sight on a loop he couldn't escape until the alarm went off.

The nightmares always started the same way.

He stands in front of a Provisions grocery store. The buff-colored stone. The green metal awning designed to look like a canvas tent. Old ladies pushing carts through the automated doors, their sustainable shopping bags folded neatly in the child seat.

He walks to the entrance, and when the doors open with a *whoosh* of noise and a wash of cool air, his right leg collapses. He drops to his left knee to clutch at the pain radiating out from his right calf as water rushes out in a frothy wave.

He stands against the flow, the pain in his leg forgotten. The aisles of produce and self-serve grains still look like Provisions, but he knows it's really the USS *Northville* inside. Sweat makes his khaki uniform stick to the skin of his back and thighs as he steps inside. The doors close behind him, and an alarm sounds from deep in the interior of the store.

He runs down the cereal aisle, but the only thing at the end is the meat counter. Grass-fed bison is on sale. A man stands at the seafood case. A thick upper body over thin bird legs, he wears Navy PT gear — short dark blue shorts and a matching t-shirt, socks pulled to his knees. Mark recognizes him as Captain Jenkins, commander of the *Northville.* The man bends over to inspect the shrimp, and blood drips from a gash over his nose, turning the ice into a crimson slush.

The sound of the alarm shifts to come from behind him, and Mark spins around. The cereal aisle is now a dark metal passageway of pipes and conduits, ending in a stairwell flooded with red flashing light.

Mark knows the explosion will be at the bottom, but he runs to it anyway. His right leg tries to unhinge, but he throws his hand to the yellow railing to steady himself. Provisions-brand puffed rice cereal scatters into the aisle in front of him, bouncing down the steps to disappear into the dark below.

He feels the texture of the thick paint under his fingers. The rising heat. The floor tilting as the *Northville* rolls into a hard starboard turn.

When the explosion comes, he is still at the top of the stairs. The red strobe becomes a swelling roar of fire, and a giant hand pushes him back to fall into the rising water behind him.

His leg feels like it's been torn from his hip. He sucks in water so hot, it's like breathing fresh coffee.

Distant screams fade into the din of waves crashing into the bulkheads of the lower passageways, and he tumbles down into the dark with the puffed rice cereal, swelling as he becomes too waterlogged to swim. The names of some of the men that died float into his mind before he can stop them. Amador, Goodwillie, Jenkins, Kennison…

The alarm by Mark's bed pounded into his dream with the driving beat of the Red Hot Chili Peppers' "Higher

Ground." It cut the names off before he could finish the mental list.

It was short a name, anyway. Mark still believed he should have died that day as well. A gunnery officer on a Navy cruiser should have known something was wrong with one of his men. Sensed the sabotage in his equipment and in his crew.

Mark sat up, but let the music continue to play as he rubbed the sleep from his eyes. He bent to work the stiffness out of his knee, extending his fingers down into the crater of missing flesh in his calf. The pins and needles in the bottom of his foot felt like creeping ants.

The houseboat rocked under him. A gentle sway caused by the wind pushing against the port side. There was supposed to be some bad weather coming. Maybe he would listen to his hangover and cancel the scheduled charter for the day. Why should somebody else care about his reputation when he didn't care about it himself?

But he got up anyway. Hard calisthenics in the early morning sun, and a shambling two-mile run. Bacon he'd smoked himself from pork loin that he got on sale at the BX two-for-one, and eggs over medium. A half a pot of coffee and one shower later, and he finally felt almost normal again as the nightmares faded into the background of his routine.

When he used to go to therapy, they told him it was his guilt that kept bringing them to the surface. Since he already knew that, he stopped going.

It didn't matter that the Government Accountability Office cleared him of any wrongdoing. They recommended retirement for Mark and the other weapons officers. He took their advice and left the Navy, but he couldn't leave the sea.

The money wasn't enough to live on, but the healthcare kept him on his feet after eighteen months of surgeries and rehab. Everybody in Key West knew what had happened to him, but none of them blamed him either.

Good friends. Brothers and sisters, every one. But sometimes, he wished one of them would say otherwise. Punish him a little so he could take a break from punishing himself.

He grabbed a trash bag and headed out to the concrete pavilion in the RV park where the other service members stayed, current members and veterans in RVs ranging from pop-up campers to rigs costing several hundred thousand dollars.

Everybody he passed waved and smiled, because how could you be sad with a view of the ocean?

He knew they had put a lot of beer and tequila away during the fish fry last night — he had started calling it the Perlmutter Memorial Barbeque, even though nobody got the joke — but the pile of cans and bottles pushed under the edge of Longjohn's rig still surprised him.

The RV was a black Newmar Dutch Star. Forty feet long, with slide-outs on both sides. The interior was nicer than many houses Mark had been in.

He finished filling the bag, then tied it off as the door opened and his friend clomped down the stairs. Dressed like he had been during the party last night, only wearing sunglasses with lenses shaped like stars. "Hey, hey!" he shouted.

Mark slung the bag over his shoulder like Santa Claus readying for a delivery. "Nice glasses."

Longjohn grinned. "You like 'em? Josie sent 'em to me."

"She the little one?"

"Six years old in two days. She said, 'Pop Pop, I found the biggest ones, but I still don't think they'll fit.' I had to bend 'em out a bit, but she was happy on the video call this morning when she saw 'em. Then, all she did was put all those filters on, though. Making herself look like a cat and shit."

Mark didn't know what that meant, but he knew if he asked, he would get a two-hour lecture on the history of phone apps.

Longjohn pulled a folding chair out from under the RV and dropped into it with a sigh. "You working today?"

The cans and bottles clinked and rattled when Mark shrugged. "I don't know. We got the storms coming in the afternoon. I didn't even want to do it when the guy called for a charter."

"What guy?"

"Just some guy wants to take his wife out. I quoted five hundred just to get him to say no, but he accepted."

"Well, now you *have* to do it. We drank that much last night."

"I guess."

Longjohn laughed. "We both know you're going to. You're an asshole, but you're a good man. Everybody sees it but you, but that doesn't make it any less true."

He put his head back to face the sky. Mark couldn't tell, but he got the feeling Longjohn had closed his eyes.

Mark chuckled with a shake of his head. "You're right about one thing. I'm gonna do it."

"What's the alternative? Going back to your houseboat and riding out the storms, while you make yourself more miserable than usual?"

Mark covered his smile with a cough. He had actually thought that exact thing. "What about you?"

"I'm doing this right here," Longjohn said. "Maybe until noon, then I got a date with Jacob to play Call of Duty before his baseball game."

Mark couldn't keep track of all the grandkids. Longjohn had about twelve of them, and all of their names started with a J. "You gonna win this time?"

"I've been practicing. Pop Pop's gonna smoke that kid."

Mark laughed, then waved as he turned to head to the dumpster. "I should be back before the storm hits."

"What am I, your mother?"

Mark had more than enough time to get the boat fueled and ready. A stop for some more beer and tequila to get ready for the storm, and it would be about time to meet one Reggie Fallon and his wife.

He turned back for a final wave, but Longjohn looked fast asleep. Mark opened his mouth to shout a goodbye, but he didn't know how to tell Longjohn how much he loved him, so he said nothing.

Chapter Six

The thought of spending the day on a stranger's boat while her husband pretended to enjoy catching bluefin made Jennifer want to fake food poisoning. She'd rather sit at home with a book, a bottle of wine, and some dark chocolate. She didn't understand Reg's supposed fascination with fishing. He spoke about it often, and he could hold a conversation about bass fishing in Ohio and salmon fishing in Alaska, but she was certain he had never baited a hook in his life.

Like all the hunting he claimed to do. She doubted if he had ever sighted down on an elk or tracked a deer through the snow. Just more lies to fill out the story he told other people about himself. Many of which she had fallen for.

If there weren't pictures of him in uniform next to the commander of a U.S. Army base in Iraq, she would have started to doubt his military history as well. How she had ever been taken in by him was a mystery.

Jennifer frowned at herself in the mirror. Now, *she* was the one lying.

She inspected her reflection. Her glutes and hamstrings felt like quivering jelly after the heavy stiff-legged deadlifts she had done that morning, but the pump helped her fill out the swimsuit, a white one-piece with a low neckline and tiny straps.

Reg liked the way she looked in the tight yoga pants she often wore, but he told her not to get too carried away or else she'd look like one of the black chicks shaking it on TikTok.

She wondered: If she had known the truth about him, would she have still gone out with him? She disappointed herself by not knowing the answer.

Reg walked into the bedroom with his jump rope draped over his shoulders. Sweat streamed down his red face and chest. The waistband of his baggy, dark gray basketball shorts was almost black with captured moisture. He threw the jump rope on the bed. "Is that the suit you're wearing?"

Jennifer looked at him through the mirror. "Yeah, why?"

"What do you mean, *why*? It was just a question."

He took his shorts and underwear off, bundling them into a ball to shoot into the hamper like it was the last shot of the game. A jumper that hit just before the buzzer. He even pumped his fist in victory when they went in without touching the sides.

He had been in good shape before, but since becoming friends with her father, there were new veins and striations appearing almost daily. He was prouder of his progress than he was of hers.

"I don't like it," he said.

She turned from the mirror. "You don't like what?"

He laughed and held his hands out like he was calming an angry dog. "Easy. The suit. I don't like it."

Jennifer thought the suit was perfect. It suited her body, and since it was a one-piece, she felt covered. She turned back around and arched her back to give him a good look at her butt. "What don't you like about it?"

Instead of taking the bait, he just smiled. "I want you to wear something more…" He rolled his hand in a circle as he searched for the right word.

"Slutty?" she asked.

"Revealing."

"So, I was right."

"Babe, no. You look fantastic in anything, but I don't want fantastic today. I want dazzling. I want amazing. I want you to distract the shit out of the guy."

"I don't understand." The charter captain? Why would Reg want him distracted?

Reg walked over and bent his knees enough to put the root of his penis against the base of her spine. She felt it start to swell, pushing into the fabric of the swimsuit.

The smell of the sickeningly sweet strawberry-watermelon pre-workout drink he used was almost strong enough to cover up the odor of his sweat as his heavy breath swept past her ear.

"Like you're distracting me right now," he said.

He'd taken the bait after all, but not like she wanted. His hands flattened out on her belly, pulling her into him. She looked into his hooded eyes and remembered why she had fallen for him. That face. That body. The way she felt when he gave her a compliment.

"Let's take a shower," he said.

"I already did."

One of his hands reached up to gently squeeze her throat. He grabbed her ponytail with the other, forcing her head back. She could think of at least five ways to break his hold, all of which ended with him on the ground writhing in pain, but she only hissed and closed her eyes, going slack in his grip.

"So take another one," he growled.

When they got into the stinging spray of the body jets, he had no problems getting it up, and he let her do whatever she wanted. Sex was the only time she was ever aggressive, and the only time he would ever allow it. The passion of the final moments was almost enough to erase all the feelings of shame and inadequacy that built up every day, but when she stood at the vanity about to blow dry her hair for the second time while he stood in the bedroom whistling merrily, she felt the stress of the last few days fall across her shoulder.

It was exhausting trying to please everyone around her all the time.

She hesitated, staring at the blow dryer hanging in front of her. She hated to use it too often. The heat damaged her hair, making it harder to keep under control in the Key West humidity. If it was up to her, she would go back to the pixie cut she had maintained for most of her life. It was easy, it suited her, and it was so much cooler than the long, thick ponytail Reg liked.

She remembered Don pretending to drown in the family pool when she was a teenager. "Save me, Tink!"

All that time on her hair, and more time on her makeup, though she wore less than Reg would like, and she was finally ready to see what he had picked out for her to wear.

He stood in front of his wardrobe mirror, wearing long board shorts and a tight swim shirt that showed off every developing ab muscle. He combed pomade into his hair like he was icing a cake. He watched her reflection to see her reaction.

A pink string bikini sat at the foot of the bed.

The comforter was as tight as smooth concrete. Reg made the bed every single day without fail. He always said it was the first battle in a daily war, so why not win it?

The feeling of material sliding up the crack of her ass never really bothered her, but it gave her a feeling of being exposed, and that put her on edge. It was tiring to constantly look around to see if she was being observed.

She put the suit on while he pretended not to watch, and she finished it with a pair of flamingo earrings and matching flip flops she thought were super cute after seeing them at Costco.

"No, no," he said. "Wear the shell earrings I got you."

She hadn't had the heart to tell him she didn't care for them when he gave them to her. He was so proud of his choice, she had claimed to love them. Now, she was caught in her own lie, but she put them on. It was one more fight avoided.

When she looked around for her purse, she saw him holding it in one hand while he dialed his cellphone with the other. She reached for it, but he held a distracted finger up, and the strap swung out of her reach. She wanted to transfer its contents into a clutch that matched her suit. One that had enough room for her money and ID, and the small Ruger LC9 handgun she never left the house without.

"Hayes?" Reg said into the phone.

Jennifer barely resisted rolling her eyes. Nelson Hayes was a man who looked like he had been built based on the blueprints of a tank. His friendly smile never seemed to touch his eyes, and she always caught him staring at her.

Reg slid the strap of her purse over his shoulder to free up his hand. He could have just handed it to her. She reached again, but he turned away with an annoyed look.

"Why are you calling Hayes?" she hissed.

He waved her off. "Did you get the other boat?"

Why did they need *another* boat?

"Check. You and the boys be ready. Wheels up in five."

This time, she *did* roll her eyes. *Wheels up.* Like driving to the marina was a critical mission.

He slid his phone into his pocket and started out of the room. She stopped him with a hand on his chest. "Can I have my purse, please?"

He pushed her hand away and cocked his hip out. He slung the purse over his shoulder. "You don't think I look pretty enough with it?"

"Reg, I want to use a different purse today. That one doesn't match."

He turned away from her reaching hand. "Black goes with everything. Come on."

"Why won't you just give me the fucking purse?" She closed her eyes with a defeated sigh. She hated losing control. "I'm sorry."

When she opened her eyes, instead of seeing his face reddening with anger, she was shocked to see him smile. He pointed at the ceiling. "Babe, it's okay. We're leaving now anyway, and you won't need a fancy purse on the boat."

"It's not fancy—"

He was already out the door.

She looked at herself in his mirror. He had forgotten to close the wardrobe door. One drawer was half out. And his damp towel was on the floor in front of the hamper.

She sighed again before tidying up, then followed him out. He was already in the Jeep. Huge tires, exposed suspension, and chromed everything. Hayes sat in a black Durango at the end of the driveway, accompanied by three other shadows. They were all Reg's old Army buddies.

When she got into the passenger seat, she looked back

to see her purse sitting open in the striped bag they always took to the beach.

He put the Jeep in gear and reached over to push her sheer white cover-up aside to drop his hand on her thigh.

An uneasy flutter settled in her guts, but she forced a smile, covering his hand with hers. The crack about her falling off the boat and dying yesterday. Wanting the guy at the boat to be distracted. The surprise sex…

Reg had unzipped her purse, and she wondered what he had been looking for. Or what he had taken out of it.

Chapter Seven

Mark thought the guy was an ape with slick hair. Almost everything he said was supposed to inspire awe in the listener, but Mark just wasn't impressed. He had been around enough men and women who had done amazing things to know how people talked about them when they were telling the truth.

He was certain that Reggie "Just Call Me Reg" Fallon was a liar.

His wife hardly talked at all. Her smile seemed perfunctory — like a bored receptionist greeting the thousandth customer of the day — and when she looked away, her mouth settled into a grim line.

As soon as he had helped her step on the boat, she swept her cover-up off, holding it out to her side, looking over her shoulder to see if he was watching. She had a touch more muscle than he usually went for, but otherwise … he had to look away to avoid being rude. The tiny bikini bottom left so little to the imagination that looking had made him feel like invading her privacy.

He still had to resist looking again, and the knowing smile on Reg's face made Mark want to punch it off.

He glanced back over his shoulder, and Mrs. Reggie was facing him, adjusting the side straps of her top. Her tits were about to spill out of the twin hankies holding them up. The sun made the intricate tattoo on her thigh — a snake winding through a design of thorns — appear to be floating above her skin.

Mark looked away again, but it wasn't the tattoo or the shadow of her nipples that stayed in his mind. It was the sadness in her eyes.

"You know," he said, putting his hands on his hips. "With the weather that's coming, I'm not sure we'll have enough time to really get a good day in. Maybe we should reschedule."

Reg paused with one foot over the rail.

"Wait a second." He pointed at the sky like he was making a point to Jesus. "I put down a deposit on your website."

Reg finished stepping aboard, and Mark held his hands up to stop him from getting any closer. "I understand, but I'm happy to refund it. I want your day to be one to remember for the *right* reasons. Not because you're puking over the side in a storm."

Reg laughed as he swept his hand past Mark's shoulder. "But we're already on board."

Based on Reg's smirk, Mark knew what he would see when he looked to where he had indicated. Mrs. Reggie was bent at the waist to spread a towel out in the same spot Nancy had used. The backs of her thighs quivered like she was having trouble holding herself in that position. The tiny triangle of pink fabric peeking out between her upper thighs made it look like she was naked.

She looked back at him, but instead of seeing a flirtatious smile, he saw near panic in her eyes. Mark looked back at Reg, but the man wasn't looking at his wife. He was looking at Mark. Like he was gauging Mark's reaction.

A nagging unease developed into an itch between his shoulders. Mark hid it with a grin he hoped looked lecherous enough to calm Reg down. "I get it. You're already here and you were hoping for a day of fishing, and though I can guarantee you'll catch more than you thought possible, the reports we've been getting all morning ... it might be best to do it another day, is all I'm saying."

Reg nodded like he was considering Mark's response. "I tell you what. I'll give you a thousand over what you quoted. Let me worry about how I'll remember it."

A thousand would go a long way toward making him feel better about being stiffed by the Perlmutters — though in reality, they had probably just simply forgotten. He had certainly been drunk enough to forget to remind them.

"I don't know. There's also possible damage to my boat if we get caught in something rough."

Reg pointed to Jesus again. "Twenty-five hundred."

Mark narrowed his eyes in thought. Why was he so intent on going? And why the weird vibes from Mrs. Reggie? Was she being abused? Trying to run?

"Fine," he said.

Reg clapped his hands, but he froze with his dopey grin spreading across his ape face when Mark held his hand up.

"But," Mark continued, "I'll need it up front."

Reg dropped his hands in defeat. "Like, I'm just supposed to have that kind of cash *on* me?"

"If you want to go out on my boat with a storm coming? Yes."

Reg's jaw bulged as he ground his teeth, but then he spread his hands with a grin that sprang up so fast, Mark wasn't sure if he had actually seen the seething anger underneath or if he had imagined it.

"I'll have to go to my Jeep. Why don't you talk to Jennifer while I get your money?"

"That her name?"

"Oh, I never introduced her?"

"No, you didn't."

"Then go shake her hand. We're all friends here."

Mark watched Reg step back on the dock and head up to the lot to the Jeep Wrangler: Tiny Penis Edition parked by the cleaning station. When he ducked inside to get his money, Mark turned to the bow.

Jennifer was in the exact position Nancy had been, but where Nancy had looked regal, Jennifer looked … ready. Tension in every muscle like she was waiting to spring.

"So, your name's Jennifer?"

"That's right." Her voice was soft and gritty, like it took force to make any sound with it. Not musical like Nancy's, but strong.

"I'm Mark Adler."

"It's nice to meet you."

"Is it?"

She sat up and spun on her towel to swing her legs over the opening to the lower deck. She kicked her feet, shielding her eyes to look up at him. "To be honest, I'm not really sure."

Mark didn't see any bruises on her skin. No swelling on her face. But something about the way she looked at her husband — and the way she looked at Mark — was turning his unease into alarm.

"Are you okay?" he asked.

Her forehead wrinkled with emotion as the corners of her mouth turned down. "I don't know."

He took a step toward her, and her face smoothed back

into the absent-minded smile. "Have you ever felt that no matter what you do, you've already fucked up so bad you'll never be right again?"

Mark looked away from her direct gaze. He heard the phantom screams of his mates dying in an explosion. Smelled the smoke. The numbing cold of the rising water. "Yes, I do."

He looked back at her as she tipped her head toward shore where Reg was straightening out of the Jeep.

"He doesn't."

Mark watched her lie back down, studying her as Reg jogged back to the dock. Perfect skin. Long blonde hair lying in a perfect tail next to her head. The sculpted muscles and the tiny bikini.

He wondered who it was all for — her, or someone else?

He knew what it was like to feel no ownership over his own life. He was a slave to his guilt. What was *she* a slave to?

"Here it is, buddy," Reg said. His eyes shone out of his red face like he had just awakened from a fever dream. A plain white envelope bulged out of his hand.

Mark tore his attention away from Jennifer to focus on Reg. He took the money with numb fingers as Reg flicked a glance out past the gap in the mangroves to the open water.

A normal gesture that suddenly looked odd.

Mark forced a smile. He took the envelope and looked inside. Without knowing what the bills were, he had no way of knowing how much was in there, but the stack seemed too thick to be just twenty-five hundred.

"What is this, all fives?"

"You can trust me."

"Says the man hoping to be trusted." Mark laughed

like it was a joke, and he put the envelope in the unlocked compartment in the control station. "I *do* trust you. I mean, we're all friends here like you said, right?"

Mark went through his usual routine of talking through the steps of casting off before getting behind the wheel and firing up the engine. The satisfying rumble rolled through him as he trolled out through the trees, and as his muscles picked his route out of long habit, he scanned the horizon.

Fewer boats than usual, but that was to be expected. There was a storm coming later, but Mark's gut tightened when he saw a boat approaching slowly from open water. Also, nothing to be worried about. It was the ocean, after all. That's where boats were *supposed* to be.

He looked at the tension building in Jennifer's body, and sweat rolled down his back between his shoulder blades. He suddenly didn't like having Reg behind him.

He hoped the storm came in sooner than expected. He could hardly wait to get the man off of his boat.

Chapter Eight

When Jennifer had first seen Mark, she had thought he was the kind of man who could be lazy because he was used to getting things with his looks. He wasn't as powerful looking as Reg, but he still looked capable. And his polite smile seemed there just to cover his pain.

Was it from the limp? Or something deeper?

His bright white compression socks were just like the ones she had seen the power lifters in her gym wear, but one of them showed off something wrong with his lower leg. Some subtle deformity she couldn't see clearly, but in spite of his limp and the occasional wince of pain, it didn't seem to limit him.

She had started to change her opinion of him when she couldn't bait him into staring at her, no matter how she stuck her ass out or pushed her tits up. He averted his gaze with a slip in his smile like it bothered him. Maybe he didn't like girls.

She enjoyed his voice, though. Assertive and confident without being overbearing. He said things with the certainty that they were right instead of how Reg said things. Like they were supposed to be right because he said so.

As they got underway, Mark held to a speed as steady as his words. He talked about the invasive species of iguanas that were killing off native plants and animals, pointing to them hanging on the limbs of the mangrove trees they passed.

Reg made a gun out of his fingers and pretended to shoot them.

Mark talked about the different fish they might see in the waters off the east coast of Key West. Where the lobsters were, and how to catch them. If she wasn't so worried about Reg's actual plans, she might have been excited to dive for some.

Mark talked about how much of Key West on this side was protected from hurricanes because of the shallow waters. Floods, on the other hand …

When the conversation turned to Mark's time serving in the Navy, Reg pretended to be interested, acting like he knew what Mark was talking about. Jennifer used the distraction to reach into the beach bag. She would claim it was for some sunscreen, but it was really to look into her purse.

"When I was on the boat, phone calls were limited," Mark said.

Jennifer snaked her hand into the purse and felt around.

"I had a girl who was a nurse on a cruise ship out of Orlando, and every once in a while, our courses would sorta coincide."

She located her wallet. Her spare set of keys. Makeup case. Tissues. Hand sanitizer. Everything she expected to be there, except for the gun.

"It was pretty special when we could hook up while I was on leave."

She felt around in the beach bag in case it just tumbled out, but she soon realized it wasn't there. She was now certain Reg had removed it. He didn't want her to be able to protect herself.

"You guys still see each other?" Reg asked. He sat with a fishing pole laying across his knees.

"Nah," Mark said. His answer made Jennifer sad, but it faded when she looked at the boat following along in the distance. Her imagination put Hayes at the helm.

She grabbed a bottle of sunscreen and sat up to face the rear of the boat. "How come?"

Mark shrugged. "You know, sometimes boats drift apart even when they're floating in the same current."

A dark cloud slid underneath the sun, and the breeze cooled. She covered her shiver by rubbing in some lotion. Reg stood up and put the pole back in its holder. He looked back at the boat closing the distance between them.

Jennifer got up and walked over to Mark while she finished rubbing her lotion in. Reg grinned at her like she was a co-conspirator and turned away to pretend he was looking at the water, but his hands were hidden in front of him.

"What's the difference between a ship and a boat?" she asked.

Mark chuckled as he turned to look behind him. Jennifer touched his arm to keep his attention on her. His eyes narrowed in concern when they met her gaze. "Well, usually, I would answer with some flippant remark about how boats carry men, and ships carry boats, but that's not technically true."

He frowned when she moved closer, putting her hand on his arm. Reg was still busy inspecting the water, his hands busy in hiding. More clouds rolled in to darken the sky further, and the wind picked up, blowing her ponytail around her shoulder to tickle her face.

"It's actually hull length and keel depth and the shape of … I was on the USS *Northville*. It was a cruiser, and we just always called it a boat."

Jennifer grabbed his arm and moved even closer. She threw her voice over his shoulder like she was playing to an invisible audience. "And how long were you in the Navy?"

"Not long enough." It was clear he wanted to see what was going on behind him, but her grip held him steady.

"What happened?"

"I was injured in an ammunition explosion." He said it like he was reciting IKEA instructions.

She pulled him to the side to put him between her and Reg.

"Is that what's wrong with your leg?" A rude question, but it focused his attention on her without alerting Reg.

He hesitated before he replied. "That's right."

"I'm sorry to hear that." She leaned out enough for one more look at Reg to make sure he wasn't paying attention. Maybe he was signaling to the other boat. She leaned back and whispered to Mark, "He is going to kill me, then his men will come for you."

Her grin felt like a silent scream, but she stepped back and dropped her hand, letting her fingers slide along his forearm. He grabbed her hand before it could fall away.

From the corner of her eye, she saw Reg turn from the water. She stepped into the space between Mark and the wheel.

"Show me how to drive," she said with a giggle.

Mark stepped back to make room. "Well, right now it's easy. Just like a car, you know? Turn right for right and left for left."

"And what if I wanted to go fast?" she purred.

She looked back to see Mark's eyes narrow in thought. Behind him, Reg smiled in approval. She saw the dark metal of the pistol flash through the air as he stuffed it into his waistband behind him.

"Looks like you were right, Mark," Reg said. "Got some weather coming in. Maybe we should catch some fish, huh?"

Mark's concern was forced away by a broad smile that took a moment to reach his eyes. He gently pulled Jennifer's hands off the wheel.

"By all means," he said. "I have just the spot."

"No," Reg said. "I think my spot is better."

Jennifer saw the bow of the boat behind them lift out of the water as it sped toward them.

Chapter Nine

A lot of men brought their wives and girlfriends on his boat. Mark couldn't put a number on the times he had been hit on. By women fawning and drunk, and sometimes by the men. Even offers to join both at the same time.

And sometimes he was tempted. Had Jennifer's advances been genuine, it would have been difficult to say no, but the fear he saw behind her act rang like a siren telling him to stop. Right. There.

He is going to kill me, then his men will come for you.

He had a gun in the locker below, various knives and tools, but nothing at hand, and Reg was looming behind him.

"A spot of your own?" Mark asked. "I thought you said you never fished out here before?"

Reg widened his stance and kept his hands behind his back like he was at parade rest. His grin looked like a dog about to bite. "No, it's a little cove coming up full of lobster."

"I don't know. I'm out here every day. Got a houseboat tied off in Sediment Key. I know just about every spot—"

"*Every* spot? Come on."

Jennifer crossed her arms and stared off the side. Mark wanted her to act a little more natural. He didn't want Reg to know she had warned him.

Reg didn't seem to notice Jennifer's change in demeanor. He pointed to an opening in the trees. "It's right up there, I think."

Mark knew the cove well. Too shallow for almost anything, and there was barely room for *his* boat since a sailboat had washed up inside, hitting the bottom and splitting open to lay over on its starboard side.

"Oh, you don't want to fish in there."

Reg pointed at the sky. "I didn't say I wanted to fish in there. I want to catch some lobsters."

"I'm telling you, there *are* no lobsters in there." Mark steered away from the cove.

Reg stepped forward so their shoulders were nearly touching. "I paid twenty-five hundred dollars. How about we just check?"

Mark still couldn't see Reg's hands. He glanced behind him to check on the other boat. It clipped over the waves on its way toward them like it was trying to outpace the coming storm. A tiny sliver of blue sky over the Gulf closed with a final push of clouds, and the day turned dark.

The sweat on his forehead cooled to a tight scour of salt. He leaned into Reg with a sly smile. "How about this? Tell your lady to move out up front where we can get a good look at her before it gets too dark."

Reg stepped away and turned to keep his back away from Mark's view. His leering grin only strengthened the predator vibes, and he nodded. "You heard him, babe. Stand up there where we can see you."

She glared at Mark as she moved to comply. She kept

her arms crossed until she stood next to her towel. It was only a few steps away from the low railing. She might have a chance to get away if anything happened.

He steered into the cove with a quick look over his shoulder. The boat following them had maybe four men on it. It steered to match his course, and Mark faced front to ease through the gap in the trees.

A solid wall of rain rushed toward them from a few miles out. He had little time to come up with a plan to get out of the trap Reg was setting.

As they cleared the mangroves, Reg turned to signal to the other boat. Jennifer stood looking out over the bow with her hands on her hips. The set of her shoulders relayed anger. Or maybe dread. Mark didn't know her well enough to interpret her body language.

He could read Reg, though. Smug satisfaction and excitement. Reg kept one hand behind his back while pointing with the other. "What's that?"

Mark followed the line of his finger to the wreck rotting on its side. Everything above the water was still stark white, but below was just a blob of shadow. The bottom was usually visible in the sun, but with the clouds, he could barely see the outline of the hull.

Were the shadows dark enough to hide a swimmer?

"Just some poor sucker that was anchored too close to the shore when the winds hit. We can get some pretty rough ones down here."

Mark pretended to be distracted by Jennifer as he shut the motor off to steer into a drift that pointed them right at the sailboat. He grabbed the tickle stick like he was ready to tease some lobster out of their holes.

He grinned at Reg. "For twenty-five hundred, I'll look for lobster in a bathtub."

Reg laughed, finally taking his other hand from behind his back. A small black pistol pointed at Mark's chest.

"Well, that is just perfect," Reg said.

The other boat appeared in the gap, and the engine revved as it fell into a slow drift. Mark felt his chance approaching.

"That's my gun," Jennifer said. She sounded offended.

Mark raised his hands. A sudden gust of wind almost took the tickle stick from his hand.

"Shut up," Reg said without looking at her. "Get down here."

"Don't do it," Mark said. "Stay right there."

Reg extended his arm like he thought it was more threatening because the gun was closer. "Shut the fuck up. All you do is talk. Jesus."

Distant lightning lit the roiling clouds like the flicker of a neon sign. The rumble of thunder matched the idling engine behind them.

Mark's boat scraped along the sandy bottom a split second before what he'd been waiting for arrived.

The other boat had stopped so hard, it had caused a wave to punch into the cove. It hit them broadside and rocked the boat up a foot before dropping it down to slam on to the shallow bottom.

With nothing to hold on to, Jennifer collapsed to her knees with a wordless shout of dismay. Reg threw his arms out for balance, staggering toward the starboard rail. Mark rode the wave and the impact with a tense core and soft knees. He stayed in position on his feet like they were still on calm seas.

The wind brought the spray of the approaching rain.

Mark swung the tickle stick before Reg could recover his balance. It cracked him on the bridge of his nose, and the impact drove him back with his arms windmilling. Reg crashed onto his ass to slide back into the transom wall.

Mark took a step to follow, but the crack of a gunshot brought him up short. A bullet struck the console next to him, sending plastic shrapnel into his face. He turned to dive into the opening leading to the lower deck, but stopped himself before he could make the steps.

His gun was down there, but there was no way out.

He looked up at Jennifer as she got off her knees and staggered back. She looked at the other boat, where the shot had come from.

He followed her gaze. One man at the helm. Three more at the bow, aiming pistols.

"Jump!" he shouted as he spun back around.

Her gaze dropped to his face, but it was like she didn't see him. Then she looked up over her shoulder, opening her mouth to shout back.

The way the boat moved under his feet told him Reg had managed to get up. Mark drove up from the deck, using the rail to pull him along toward where Jennifer stood. A quick look back showed him Reg bringing his gun around for a shot of his own. His gritted teeth were red from the blood gushing from the gash across his nose.

A pop of sound followed by a burning along his ribs, and Mark lowered his shoulder with a silent apology. He blasted into Jennifer, driving the scream right out of her as his tackle drove her over the rail and into the air.

More gunfire, and the roar of wind passing by his ears. The slap of crashing into the shallow water, and he rolled as they went under to take the impact of the bottom against his back instead of landing on top of her. He dug his fingers into the sandy, churning as much of it as he could as he kicked into a struggling swim. Jennifer clung to him, her face pressed into his chest. Her legs flailed out behind them as he dragged her toward a break in the sail-boat's hull.

The pressure of the water was raw noise against his ears, but the boat's motor and the bubbles weren't enough to cover up his pounding heartbeat. Then a new sound filled in the spaces. The crescendo of the rain finally making it to the cove.

Chapter Ten

The gunshot made Jennifer gasp in shock, but Mark's tackle knocked the air back out of her. She folded over his shoulder as they flew out over the water. They rotated like a spinning arrow.

She managed a shallow breath against his arms crushing her ribs, and she rode him into the water. Her face hit flat on the surface, and saltwater blasted up her nose and down her throat. She panicked as they hit the bottom and pushed a cloud of sand up around them.

She clawed and kicked, desperate for air, as he pulled her through the water. It sounded like a howling wind whipped past her ears.

In spite of the salty burn, she kept her eyes open, but all she could see was the increasing dark. She fought against him, but his embrace was a straitjacket.

A sharp sting just above her hip became a searing trail all the way down the side of her thigh to her knee, and the darkness became absolute. She reached for his face to dig her thumbs into his eyes, but before she could find them, they burst out of the water.

Jennifer pulled in a breath that felt like fire, only to cough it out again as he pulled her to a rough angled ledge. She held onto it as if the water was a bottomless pit instead of a few feet deep. He put his hand over her mouth, and she coughed into his palm. She grabbed his wrist with both hands, but she didn't pull it away. She held it until she could hold a breath without her diaphragm going into spasms, and she finally heard his soft voice above the sizzle of rain.

"Shhh, it's okay. Breathe. Just breathe."

She turned away from his hand. Dim light from above reflected off the rippling water. A dark wall slanted away from her.

"We're in the sailboat." Her voice sounded like a small dog growling at an intruder.

Mark dropped down into the water so their eyes were level. Tiny cuts on his left cheek and over his eye seeped with blood. "It's the only place I could think to go."

"Where's Reg?"

"I don't know. Let me squeeze past you, and I'll find out."

Gunfire rattled across the water. The wet air zinged as bullets tore open the side of the boat they hid inside. Bright holes punched through the splintering wood a foot over her head. Mark lunged to cover her with his body, and her head cracked off the soggy wall behind her.

When the gunfire stopped, he stayed pressed against her. He put his mouth near her ear and whispered, "We need to get out of here."

"How?"

"I've been on this boat before. Salvage is illegal, but looking can't hurt anybody, right?"

That sounded like a rationalization to her. "I guess not."

"The only way out is through the lower quarters up to the deck."

"Like, the deck of the boat that is exposed to the gunfire?"

"Yep, but it also means we have to go a bit underwater."

She struggled to get a deep breath under his weight. "Can you get off me?" she hissed.

"I'm sorry."

He tensed to move, but more gunfire made him drop back down. The edge of the opening below her dug into her lower back.

Reg's voice cut through the noise of the storm. "Here's what's gonna happen!"

"He sounds pissed," Mark whispered. His matter-of-fact tone almost made her break with laughter.

"You're gonna come out, or we're gonna keep lighting this boat up until there's nothing left but wet sawdust."

"He'll kill us anyway," Mark warned.

"No shit."

She pushed against him, and he rolled away, pulling her into the water next to him. Her toes could just touch the bottom. She held onto his shoulder to keep from going under.

Another round of gunfire sent more rounds shredding through the hull. A bullet struck the water next to her head. Another sank into the wood over her shoulder. She looked at the light glittering in Mark's eyes. "You know the way?"

He nodded.

She closed her eyes. "How far is it?"

"What, like how long do you have to hold your breath?"

"Yeah."

"I won't be swimming. Just pulling us along with my hands, but I won't be able to see. Maybe forty-five seconds?"

"You have thirty seconds!" Reg shouted.

"Fine, if you're going to be pushy," Mark said with a bitter sneer.

She couldn't help it this time. She slapped her hand over her mouth to stifle the squeal of laughter that turned into a gagging cough. Mark waited until she caught her breath.

"Sorry," he said.

She shook her head as she used his shoulder to pull herself behind his back. She wrapped her arms around his chest and put her cheek against his shoulder blade. "Let's do it."

Mark pushed away from the wall to float in the water. "Big breath on three. One … two…"

She filled her lungs on the last number and closed her eyes. He plunged them both into the dark.

The muscles in his back and shoulder bunched against her as he pulled them along. She could tell her short nails were digging into his skin, but she couldn't stop.

Her lungs and throat already burned from sucking in water when they went under the first time, but something about knowing she had to hold her breath — even if it was just less than a minute — made her chest ache. Her throat locked and trembled, and the air pushed her cheeks out until she finally opened her lips and exhaled.

Now the desire to inhale was a scream of anguish in her mind. She raked her nails across his chest like claws, and she kicked her feet, banging her knees against the backs of his legs. She wanted air and light.

The sound of splashing water echoing back to her ears was the first sign that they had made it. The second was

Mark flinging her from his shoulder with a growl. He put his hands on his chest.

"Jesus, I thought you were trying to rip my heart out."

She held onto something oily and slick as she caught her breath. "I'm sorry," she rasped. "I don't often swim in dark water while my husband tries to kill me."

"Well, it's new for me, too."

The rain pounded on the hull, already louder than when it started a few minutes ago. If Reg wanted to shout at them now, she didn't think they would hear it.

She looked around with a squint to pick details out of the shadows. They were next to a set of broken stairs angling up to the slope of the ceiling. Rain poured in through the open hatch leading to the main deck of the sailboat. She could see the dark storm overhead.

Mark slogged over to stand under it. He put one foot on the part of the stair rail still intact and pushed himself up to look over the bottom edge of the hatch.

"It looks like he's looking around my boat for something."

"The money," she said.

"Yep. He took it out of the console and put it in his trunks like he's trying to smuggle it out of prison."

She stifled more laughter as she looked for a way to get next to him for a look of her own.

"It looks like he's shouting at the guys on the other boat. There doesn't to seem to be anybody piloting."

She climbed up on the edge of a table. It bent under her but held her weight. She grabbed Mark's leg for stability, and he reached down to give her a hand, but she still couldn't see over the edge.

She growled in frustration and dropped back into the water at the bottom of the stairs.

"What is going on, anyway?" Mark asked. "Why does he want to kill you?"

"He wants my shares of my parents' company, but Don won't give it to him."

"Who's Don?"

"My father."

"You call your father Don?"

"Is that important?" She looked up at him and noticed the blood staining his shirt from just under his pec to his waist. She pointed. "Did I do that?"

He glanced down before shaking his head. "No, it's where he shot me."

"What?" She lunged forward to attempt another climb for a better look, but he waved her down.

"Hang on. He's climbing over from my boat to the other one. They're not firing or anything. He's just talking to the other three."

Jennifer froze. "Three?"

"Yeah, but it's kind of dark and tough to see."

"There should be four of them. Four men *and* Reg. Where's the other guy?"

A wave exploded from the water's surface next to her as something rose out of it in a rush. A man dressed in a St. James dark gray utility shirt. He held a knife out in front of him as he wiped water from his eyes.

Here was the other guy.

Chapter Eleven

Mark watched Reg lean in to talk to his men, shouting over the noise of the storm. He just wanted to kill his wife to get her part of the company? Why involve Mark?

He looked down at Jennifer to ask what was going on again when the water next to her exploded upward to become a man holding a knife. Mark let go to fall back to the bottom of the stairs, but Jennifer jumped forward with a ragged scream.

Mark cursed himself as he landed with the stair rail between him and Jennifer's attacker, but before he could push through the water to help, she had moved in under the guy's swinging knife to launch a punch into his throat.

He remembered how her arms had tried to crush the breath out of him when he was pulling her through the water. She was stronger than she looked.

The guy fell back to slam into the wall with a choking gasp, but when Jennifer rushed in to grab his wrist, the guy brought a leg up to put his boot in her stomach. She bent over it with an explosive breath, and the guy shoved her back.

She skipped across the water to crash into the broken railing. It tore free and splashed down on top of her, pushing her into the dark water. Mark jumped forward to grab her flailing hand, but the knife swiped through the air an inch in front of his fingers.

He snatched his hand back as the guy recovered from his miss and turned to face him. Mark splashed water up into the guy's face, and when he flinched back, Mark jumped in to lay his elbow into the guy's jaw. The guy's head snapped back into the wall, and he slumped to sputter blood into the water.

Mark spun back to grab the splintered railing off Jennifer. He threw it aside and pulled her out of the water, but when she hit the surface, she connected with a wild punch to his left cheek. The panicked shot caught him off guard, and he fell back, dragging her under again.

She screamed and thrashed, but he managed to get his arms around her, throwing his head back to keep from catching her forehead into his nose.

"It's me, it's me!" he shouted.

"Who's me?"

"Hey, he's trying to kill me too, okay?"

She stiffened in his arms. When she looked up into his face, she tensed again, but this time her struggle was to get away instead of hurting him.

"Let go of me!"

Mark opened his arms and stepped back, giving her room. She looked around like she was trying to find something to kick. Mark pointed at the guy snoring bubbles into a pink froth.

"Who the fuck is that guy?"

"Mitch Borning. One of Reg's army buddies working for my father. They call him Mitbo." She snarled as she turned away to look up through the hatch. "They always laugh at his dumb jokes, but I think he's an asshole."

Mark bent to fish around in the water for the dropped knife. When he found it, he stood to hold it up like he had won a prize.

"Me too," he said.

"You too, what?"

"I also think he's an asshole."

He held the knife in his teeth, resisting the urge to *aargh* like a pirate, and pulled the broken railing over the edge of the table Jennifer had tried to climb on.

"What are you doing?"

He pulled the knife free. "They think their guy is on here, so they won't shoot, right? At least, not right away. We can get outside on the deck and swim away."

"To where?"

"To land. It's only a few yards away from us. We might be spotted, but maybe they don't want to risk killing the asshole here."

He climbed up to balance on the railing. He grabbed the edge of the hatch.

"Come on. Use me to climb—"

Before he could finish, she jumped up and latched on, using his shoulders and hips as footholds. Like a spider monkey, she scampered up his body and out the hole to roll down the slanted deck and into the water.

"Okay, then." He stabbed the knife into the wood under the hatch so he could get a grip on the edge with both hands. He pushed off the rail and pulled himself up so he could get one arm thrown over onto the deck.

His lower body swung helplessly as he tried to find something to grab. Jennifer slid out of the water and pressed against the deck. She reached for Mark's hand, but just as he grabbed her wrist, something grabbed one of his legs and dragged him back through the hatch.

The combined weight of Mark and Mitbo pulled Jennifer up the slope with a scream. Mark tried to let go, but Jennifer held fast, and there was no fighting gravity. As he fell back on top of Mitbo, Jennifer slipped over the edge like running water.

Mark pulled her back inside the sailboat, and they landed in a thrashing pile. Mark rolled away, pulling Jennifer with him, and Mitbo stood to sling water from his dripping hair. Blood poured from his mouth, and his jaw sat crooked, jutting out to the side.

Mark moved to engage him, and Jennifer finally let go. The water swirling around his thighs made it difficult to climb the slanted floor, and he was unable to dodge Mitbo's first blow, a glancing shot over his left eyebrow,

Mark took the shot and moved in to slam the top of his head into Mitbo's chin. He grunted from the impact but didn't drop, so Mark swung a right into his ribs. A left up into his liver. The blows slowed him down but didn't stop him.

A return flurry of punches hit Mark in the collarbone and forehead, pushing him back to regroup, but the back of his knees hit the sharp edge of the broken railing, and he folded up to collapse backward.

He rolled over to his hands and knees to get his head out of the water, and he felt weight on his back. A foot planted in the middle of his shoulder blades. He looked back to see it was Jennifer.

She screamed as she pushed off of him, and he rolled to the side to watch her rise, stretched out toward the edge of the hatch. He thought she had used him to springboard up to grab the edge and pull herself back out, but as

Mitbo's shadow descended on him, he saw her grab the knife he had stuck in the wood.

It came down in her hand as she landed. Mark couldn't look away from the fury on her face.

Mitbo grabbed Mark's throat with his left hand and drew his right back to score a knockout, but another scream brought him up short. His eyes flicked to his left to see Jennifer coming, but it was too late. She brought the knife up in an arc that ended with the blade planted in his neck.

Mitbo lurched back with his eyes wide with shock and pain. He reached up for the hilt as he dropped to his knees. Jennifer stared at him in horror, heaving with exhaustion and emotion.

Mark stood up and kicked the knife with his heel, driving it in deeper and pushing Mitbo back to splash into the water.

He jumped over to put himself between Jennifer and the man she had helped kill.

"Hey!" he shouted into her face. She blinked and looked at him like she was meeting him for the first time. "We still have to get out of here. Do you want to climb or swim?"

Rain fell into her face, but she seemed not to notice.

"Climb."

He pulled her away from the floating body and grabbed the chunk of railing again. Using the same method as before, he held the edge of the hatch while she climbed out onto the deck. It was much harder pulling himself up this time, but she was there to grab his arm. They tumbled down the deck into the water, and in a flash of lightning, he saw Reg and his men leaning against the railing of their boat.

Bullets struck the deck around the edges of the hatch,

and Mark pulled Jennifer back under. She didn't fight him, and he dragged her around the bow of the sailboat, ducking under the decorative prow.

With the boat between them and the gunfire, Mark crawled out of the water to pull her to shore. Once up on the rocky sand, he dropped down and flopped onto his back. Her knee grazed his balls as she fell on top of him, but when he opened his mouth to say something, his mouth filled with rain.

He turned his head to the side as she settled onto his chest. He didn't know how *she* felt, but he was suddenly so tired, if somebody stepped around the boat to shoot them, he might just let them. He shielded her eyes with one hand and reached down to rub his knee with the other. If the throbbing was anything to go by, it wouldn't last much longer.

Chapter Twelve

The storm had made Reg so wet, he might as well have jumped in after Jennifer like Mitbo had. He pulled the envelope out of his shorts and handed it to Hayes. The big man took it without comment and dropped it into his cargo pocket.

"You think Mitbo took care of it?" he asked.

Johnson, a man that Hayes liked but Reg hated — with his perfect smile and hair that wasn't thinning at the crown — peered into the driving rain. "I can't tell no more. I think *something* is going on over there, but I ain't sure."

Reg squinted into the storm. There was just enough light behind the clouds to see by, but the details were obscured by raindrops. He cocked his ear. Was that a scream?

The third man stepped up to stand at Reg's shoulder. Reg thought his name was Anderson, but he couldn't be sure. Hayes had hired him, and Reg barely remembered him from when they were stationed together in Iraq. He was one of the boys. Slick bald head, and his usually curled mustache hung down like soaked squirrel tail.

"It was her," Anderson said. "She popped out of the hatch, but somebody dragged her back in."

"Was it Mitbo?" Reg asked.

"Don't know."

"Fuck!" Reg stomped away from the rail. "I need to start making calls."

Hayes pulled his phone out and shielded the screen from the rain.

Johnson held his hand up to block the light and averted his eyes. "Jesus, you wanna blind us so we can't see in the dark no more?"

"You aren't calling *anybody* right now," Hayes said. "No signal."

Reg stowed his phone and went back to the boat controls.

"You think it was the storm?" Reg asked.

Hayes nodded and pointed to shore. "Check it out."

Reg spun around, expecting to see Jennifer and Mark running away, but he only saw a wall of darkness.

"What? Check *what* out?"

"No lights," Hayes said.

It took a moment for Reg to understand what his friend was saying. Except for the emergency beacons in the airfields, he didn't see any lights on land.

"It knocked the power out?" Reg shouted. "How bad was this storm supposed to be?"

Hayes shrugged. He looked like a man standing in line at the DMV instead of a killer waiting for his shot.

"Pretty bad," he said.

"I see something," Johnson said.

Reg rushed back to the rail. "What?"

"It's the guy. And Jennifer. They're on the deck, but I don't see Mitbo."

Reg raised his pistol and emptied the magazine in the

direction of where he remembered the hatch being located. As he reloaded, he looked at the questioning faces of his men. "Come on. If they got out, then Mitbo is gone. Let's put some hate into the Navy boy's boat."

He turned to aim at Mark's engine, and the other three joined him. Two Glocks and an AR-15. He doubted if anybody would hear a single shot in the cacophony of the storm. But even in the heavy rain, he saw the sparks under the engine cover.

He turned away and pulled Anderson back from the rail. He didn't bother with Johnson.

The fuel line exploded with a crushing *whump* of sound that pushed a sheet of rain into his back. Gas-soaked debris fell all around, only to gutter out after hitting the water.

Reg turned toward Anderson. "You and Johnson jump in and wade to shore, see if you can spot 'em anywhere."

"They could be a half mile away," Anderson whined.

"Yeah, or they could be waiting behind the boat for us to leave."

"So, then what?"

"Seriously? *Kill* them. Me and Hayes will go back and report to Harbor Patrol that my wife and Mitch Borning, one of her employees, enlisted the help of a fishing charter captain to take me out and kill me at sea."

"Why would she do that?" Anderson asked.

"Because they were having an affair, and I found out."

"But Mitbo was married."

"So fucking what? Married men fuck around all the time."

"Yeah, but his wife is pretty cool."

"I don't give a shit. Look at this." Reg pointed to his swelling nose. "They even broke my nose, right? Between that, our story, and whatever they find in this mess, I think they'll believe it."

Anderson looked away. "Whatever."

Reg looked to Hayes but got no support. He holstered his pistol. "Just go. Find them, and kill them, but try to make it look like you did it in self-defense."

Anderson swung his leg over the railing. "Sure thing. How about to make it look *really* good, we give them each a gun?"

"Jesus, will you shut up?" Reg signaled for Hayes. "Come around a little closer to the shore so they can get out."

Hayes guided the boat back out into the slightly deeper water in the gap between the mangroves. The boat scraped along the chunks of concrete that made up much of the outer shore.

Anderson and Johnson hopped off and clambered over the slick debris to solid ground. They dropped into a crouch to disappear into the bushes.

"Let's fuck off," he said.

Hayes brought the boat around and guided them back along the route Mark had taken them. "You know where you're going?"

"Not really. It's dark as shit."

"Just get me back to the marina so I can get the tracker out of the Jeep. We should be able to see where she is using the locator in her earrings. And you know the best part?"

Hayes seemed unamused, but Reg had never really seen him smile. "Tell me."

"She *hated* those earrings the second I gave 'em to her. She acted like she loved 'em, but I can tell. They *all* lie."

Hayes grunted. A sound Reg had come to recognize as laughter.

"But soon, I won't have to worry about her anymore.

I'll have her share of St. James. The *majority* share, and we'll just push Don and Janet out on their ass to sink with their daughter, and then we'll have it *all.*"

Hayes nodded like he had heard some special wisdom. Reg dropped into the wet seat across from the controls. He had no idea how Hayes was finding his way. He couldn't even see the shore anymore.

"When we get back, get a new team ready." All this shouting was making his throat hurt.

"You got it."

"And when you can, make some calls. I want our story out there as soon as we can get it."

Hayes didn't answer this time. Reg didn't mind. He was used to being ignored.

Chapter Thirteen

The news had said the storms weren't going to last long, but they were going to be powerful. Mark usually never paid that much attention to the forecast. Sometimes it was a lot like asking the Magic 8 Ball.

"Will it rain today?"

Shake shake shake.

— The chances are good. —

Fresh gunfire sounded like distant fireworks in the din of the howling wind and driving rain. Jennifer lifted her head from his chest with a groan. "What are they shooting at now?"

Mark heard somebody *whoop* with excitement. He pushed off the ground to sit up, lifting Jennifer along with him.

"I don't know, but it sounds like they're having fun."

Using his shoulders as support, Jennifer rose to her knees, but she stopped there as if she didn't have the energy to make it all the way to her feet. An angry scrape from her hip down to the back of her knee cut through some of the thorns in her tattoo. Blood seeped from dozens of cuts on her elbows and hands.

Sudden light burned his vision into a white haze. He squinted away from the bright flare of an explosion a split-second before feeling the blast ripple through the ground. He threw himself against Jennifer, but instead of going down under his weight, she held him up. She shouted into his ear, "Will you stop doing that!"

He pulled away to look back over his shoulder. Burning debris trailed through the rain like lazy comets. "*That's* what they were shooting."

"What?"

"My boat." He looked back at her, and his vision blurred from tears instead of rain.

"Why? To keep us from getting away?"

His sorrow was unreasonable, but he couldn't stop it. "It didn't deserve any of this."

He remembered when he'd bought it. Drove up to Alabama to get it off a retired Army drill instructor. Pulled it out of the lake and toasted the purchase with a couple of beers on the guy's dock. Tony Weber was his name. Dead from prostate cancer a month later.

"You're bleeding."

He watched Jennifer shuffle closer to reach for the bottom of his shirt.

"We should get out of here," he said.

"Take your shirt off."

He pulled it over his head with a wince. The cold rain hitting the bloody furrow along his ribs was like alcohol on a burn. She pulled the wet shirt from his hands and balled it up to jam it into the wound like it was going to be able to soak up more fluid.

He tried to pull away, but she held him fast with her other hand on his hip to provide pressure.

"Seriously," he said. "We need to leave."

She looked up at him in annoyance. "Then hold this."

She let go without seeing if he would take over. She stood up to splash along the bottom of the sailboat until she could peek around the stern. Mark dropped the shirt behind him and followed her.

Like a scene from a Scooby Doo cartoon, he put his head on top of hers to sneak a look of his own.

Through the dying flames of what was left of his boat, Reg talked to three men on the deck of the other boat that had followed them. One pale gorilla and two smaller guys, and they looked like they were arguing about something important. Mark could hear the voices but not the words.

"He's pissed about something," Jennifer said.

"I think I broke his nose."

"That would probably do it."

"And we kinda got away."

"That too."

"And he's an asshole."

"Tell me about it."

Mark pulled back and looked down at her. "How long were you married?"

"Fourteen months."

"You measure your marriage in months, like you would a toddler's age? Twenty-four months instead of two years?"

She looked up at him in confusion. "What?"

He looked back toward the boat. "Nothing."

The motor revved, and the boat backed up in a slow circle toward the rubble and concrete debris that lined the side of the cove entrance.

"What are they doing now?" Jennifer asked.

"Probably gonna drop off a guy to come find us."

The two men who had been arguing kicked out over the railing and dropped onto the broken concrete that made up the shore. A few crouched steps away from the water, and they disappeared into the bushes under the mangrove trees.

"Shit," Jennifer whispered.

Mark grabbed her shoulders and eased her back behind the boat. He looked back into the trees as the sound of the boat's motor receded into the growling wind. "How do you feel about crocodiles?" he asked.

Jennifer grabbed his arm like she wanted to pull it off. "What do you mean?"

"I think they'll try to flank us if we stay. Or chase us if we run inland." Except for the blinking red beacons of the Naval Command airstrips, he couldn't see any other lights. "The power must be out all over. I can't see shit."

"What do you mean, am I afraid of crocodiles?"

"That's not what I asked."

He felt her shiver. Her lower lip quivered as she waited for a better answer. Her skin felt cool and clammy.

"I'm sorry," he said. "Your husband's men are going to try to flank us or catch us."

"Then why all that about crocodiles?"

"Because we have to move, and the only way is inland, where the crocodiles are."

She stared into the dark with wide eyes.

He pulled her up on a chunk of concrete. "They're all over these inlets and coves. Hell, sometimes they get into people's swimming pools and eat their dogs."

"They eat their *dogs*?"

"Look, we've stayed here long enough. There ain't much of it, but the pink in your suit is pretty easy to spot in the dark."

"But they eat dogs."

"People too. It's die by bite or by bullet. You pick."

"I don't want to die at all."

"Staying here will get us killed for sure. At least if we move, we have a chance, right?"

She waited so long that he was about to throw his hands up in disgust.

"What if we do both?" she asked.

"What, like split up?"

"Yeah, what if I stay hidden while they come to this location? But you go to where they went into the weeds and follow them."

If it worked, maybe they would end up with weapons. Or they could stay hidden until the storm broke. Or … he shrugged. "I don't hate it." He swept his hand at the piles of concrete surrounding the cove. "Find a spot, and with any luck, I'll see you in a few minutes."

She nodded before spinning and scrambling through the debris. Mark didn't wait for her to get situated before moving out in a crouch in the opposite direction. About fifteen yards later, he cut into the bushes, crawling along the rough ground at the base of the mangroves. He didn't bother trying to be quiet. He couldn't hear anything over the storm. He doubted anybody else could, either.

Nearby gunshots made him freeze. He eased his head out of cover to see sparks ignite off the concrete around Jennifer's hiding spot. Had they seen her, or were they just guessing and hoping to get lucky?

More sparks a few yards south, and bullets chunked into the bottom of the sailboat.

So they *were* guessing. Good.

He ducked back into the bushes and moved toward the muzzle flashes. He had wasted time in the water. They should have been a half a mile away by now.

But if things were so dire, why did he feel so good?

Chapter Fourteen

Jennifer tried squeezing into a hole in the concrete pile, but a flash of a crocodile's snout in her mind made her draw back. A shudder of fear made her teeth clack together.

She could handle men trying to kill her. Men brandishing knives and guns. Freezing cold rain and unsettling darkness. What she couldn't stand was the thought of getting attacked by an alligator. Or a crocodile.

And maybe a man's disapproval. She couldn't stand that either.

She sat back and hugged herself as shame rose up to fight with her fear. She made her hands into fists and pressed them into her temples. This was not the time to fall apart.

Gunfire cracked out of the darkness like a counterpoint to the constant rumbling of the clouds. A ricochet on the chunk she hid behind sent concrete fragments stinging across her back.

She dove to the side, scraping across jagged edges until her hands found the water again. Did crocodiles like water? She was sure of it. More bullets hit a few yards away, and she flattened herself into the thin sand between the concrete and the cove.

The splash of weight hitting the water behind her. She craned her neck around to look. The sparkle of water glistening off craggy skin. A hissing rumble so low she felt it in her bones.

Her mind lit with terror and panic, every muscle tightened into immobility. They had spoken her fear into existence. A crocodile sat half in the water, its tail trailing up onto the pile of concrete she had just been hiding behind.

She felt the scream bubbling up into her throat before she could stop it. When the croc opened its mouth, it was like it had her voice.

She scrambled up out of the water with her upper body twisted so could see behind her, but three steps into her escape, she ran into somebody.

She could only use noises to express the horror of what followed her along the sand as she thrashed against him. One of Reg's men, and she couldn't remember his name.

He grabbed her around the waist and flung her away. She came up sputtering to point at the crocodile as it took a tentative step toward the man's position.

He pointed a pistol at her face. "Where's the other one, bitch?"

Before she could shout a warning, Mark burst out of the bushes to put his shoulder into the man's ribs. The guy *whuffed* out a surprised breath when he came off his feet. His gun sailed up in a flashing arc to land a few feet in front of her. She barely saw it, since her gaze was glued to the croc slowly advancing along the shore.

Mark landed on top of the guy, but when he rose up to fight, the guy threw him aside to scramble backward for the gun. The other guy rushed out with his pistol moving back and forth between Jennifer and Mark. Her mind screamed his name at her. *Anderson!*

That meant the first one was Johnson. They were almost always together. Like brothers ... or lovers, maybe?

She tore her gaze from the croc to watch Anderson try to cover them both at once as Johnson reached to retrieve his weapon. The sound of the crocodile's jaws snapping over Johnson's forearm brought her attention right back.

The croc dropped into a roll, but instead of going along with it, Johnson's arm twisted with a wet snap. Johnson screamed and fell forward as the croc thrashed into another spin. Anderson jumped back with a shout and unloaded into the croc's neck under its jaw and down its belly.

The croc let go with a hiss and flopped over to dig its claws into the sand. It made a gurgling sputter as it crawled away, but Jennifer thought it had less energy than before, and in just a few steps, it stopped to slap into the water with a final sigh.

Johnson sat up to cradle his mangled arm in his lap. He took a deep breath, then screamed as he stared at the bloody mess.

Anderson took a hesitant step in the croc's direction, but his progress was stopped dead when Mark ran out of the water to tackle him into the rough concrete. The sound of Anderson's head bouncing off the pile was almost as bad as the sound of Johnson's arm ripping from its socket.

Jennifer leaned to the side to throw up in the water, but nothing came out except burning acid. She had been too anxious all day to eat. She remembered Reg eating a hearty breakfast, though. The thought of the greasy bacon he'd scooped gravy up with made her heave again.

She scrubbed her face and looked at the two men struggling above her. Anderson's face was a torn mask of blood, but he still fought, broken teeth clenched in effort. He had Mark by the throat with one hand, while the other pounded at Mark's face and shoulder like a mallet.

Mark reeled back and swatted Anderson's hands away before bringing his elbow down in a strike that sent blood flying into the air.

Jennifer looked away to see Johnson's gun sitting in the sand. She glanced up at Johnson, and he looked up from his lap like he felt her watching him. He looked into her eyes before flicking his gaze over to the gun. Then they looked at each other again.

She saw him tense just before she dug in to dive for the gun herself. Their heads *whocked* together right as they landed. Her fingers filled with grit while his came up with the gun. She blinked the pain and light of the collision away and grabbed his wrist with both hands.

She rolled over him to slam his hand into the ground, and the gun popped out. She let go to reach for it, and he grabbed her by the throat. With a cry of effort, he jerked her up and flipped her back until her head and shoulders slapped into the sand and rocks.

Jennifer gasped for air, her breaths stifled by the fingers tightening around her neck. As he pressed down relentlessly, blood from his wounded arm streaked across her face, momentarily blinding her.

She threw her hips up again to lift him off, making space between them, and she reached down to grab a handful of his balls. He grunted and fell forward, but he didn't let go. She squeezed until her forearm cramped, but he still held on. Spots floated in front of her eyes, blocking out the sight of his agonized face.

She reached blindly with her other hand, dragging her fingers down his useless arm. Then she grabbed his mangled forearm and pulled like she wanted to rip it off.

He finally let go and rolled away from her with a fresh scream. He landed on top of the gun, but she couldn't do anything about it. She was too busy trying to get fresh air into her bruised throat.

The coughing fit made her heave again. This time, she tasted both bile and blood. Was it hers, or had some of his dripped into her mouth? The thought brought fresh spasms, but she clamped down and forced herself to her feet.

Above her, Mark straddled Anderson. They both breathed like they had just run a marathon. Anderson reached up to grab at Mark's bare skin. Mark pulled his fist back for another blow.

Jennifer looked away before it could land to see Johnson reaching behind his back for the pistol. He shouted in triumph and pulled it out from under him. Jennifer crossed the gap between them and dropped both of her knees on his chest, driving all her weight down.

Something in his torso cracked, and his shout trailed off into a liquid whine.

She fell off to land on his hand that still held the gun. She dug at it until he let go. His reaching fingers grabbed the tiny strap of her bikini top. He stared up into the rain as he choked to death fighting the broken bones in his chest. She couldn't stand to hear the wet gasping as he tried to breathe.

Jennifer put the gun to Johnson's cheek and squeezed the trigger.

The temple on the other side of his face split open in a wash of blood and bone, and the eye bulged out like something was pushing on it from behind. She dropped the gun and screamed into her hands. She closed her eyes, but she could still see his dead face.

Scraping footsteps behind her, and she let her hands

fall to look over her shoulder. Mark staggered over to drop into the sand next to her. "It was 'Deacon Blues,'" he said.

She pulled her strap back up and ran her hands over her thighs like she was smoothing her skirt. "What?"

"The song that Harold was whistling when he left yesterday. It just now popped into my mind. 'Deacon Blues' by Steely Dan."

She had no idea who that was. "Is he any good?" Her voice sounded like a rusty saw blade.

"When we get out of this, I'll play it for you, and you can tell me."

"Okay."

Jennifer thought about her Grandma Jean. It had been years since that sweet old woman had come to mind.

She had met her husband just a few months after the Korean War. A man named Gene St. James. He had often told the story about how they had met. How he wanted to buy that *little blonde* at the drugstore a drink.

They shared the same first name and a passion for life, so why not share a last name, too. They were married within the month.

Mama Jean and Papa Gene had six kids. Don was the youngest, and the last to have kids of his own. By the time Jennifer was born, the couple had long since become Grandma Jean and Grandpa Gene.

Janet had inherited a lot of funny old sayings from *her* family, but none of them topped what had come out of Grandma Jean's mouth.

"That girl's like a fart on a hot skillet."

"Time means nothing to a pig."

"Come the revolt, there'll be no television."

"There she is, standing with one arm as long as the other."

Jennifer never bothered to figure out what they meant.

They were just things Grandma Jean said sometimes. That, and the dancing.

She and Grandpa Gene danced most weekends. For forty-five years of a fifty-two-year marriage — other than bowling — it was the only thing they did. Vacations in the Buick Roadmaster. Many evenings down at the Legion. USO parties and VA benefits. But always dancing.

Jennifer remembered the huge stack of Lawrence Welk albums in their basement — the site of many family parties. Standing on Grandpa Gene's feet as he spun her around, making the dark paneling and shag carpet a blur around her.

And music. There was always music in their house. From when they lived in Springfield, Ohio across from the old Kroger to when they moved into the bungalow Don bought them in Key Largo. Grandma Jean turned her nose up at the changing fads of modern pop, but Jennifer had caught Grandpa Gene bobbing his head to a Justin Timberlake song. She couldn't remember which one.

Grandpa Gene must have been in his eighties by then. A sheepish smile, and he patted Jennifer's shoulder. "Jeanie won't dance to it, but it doesn't mean I can't listen."

When he got cancer from over four decades of smoking, Grandma Jean went with him to chemo. Held his hand, and they rocked back and forth accompanied by her humming. When the treatment was deemed unsuccessful, he came back home to die in his own bed. The record player ran nearly non-stop, and most days would find Grandma Jean next to his bed, holding his hand and humming along.

When Grandpa Gene passed, his family watched her go to the record player. She put the tonearm back, slid the record — Tom Jones — into its sleeve, and she closed the lid. She never turned it on again.

A week later, Jennifer asked why she never listened anymore. Grandma Jean had poured the second cup of regular coffee for the day before switching to decaf. "Because without your grandfather to hear it, it wouldn't be the same. After a thing has changed, it can't ever go back. Not ever."

Jennifer had always scoffed at that notion of finality. It felt too much like fate. Like what people told themselves when they couldn't do something. "It is what it is," they'd say.

She wiped dripping water from her eyes and glanced over at the dark lump of shadow several yards away. The man she had killed.

She suddenly knew what Grandma Jean was trying to tell her. Something had changed, and Jennifer couldn't imagine *any* music sounding good ever again.

Chapter Fifteen

Mark had been working on his guy when he'd heard the gunshot, but the guy wouldn't quit. Just kept taking punishment and throwing a good shot of his own every once in a while.

Mark's hands hurt. His shoulders ached. He could barely get a breath. And still the guy fought back.

When Jennifer had shot the other guy, Mark had looked around, afraid he'd see her dead, but before he could make sense of what was behind him, his guy popped him on the point of his chin with a killer shot. It didn't have a lot behind it, but it was placed perfectly. Mark fell back as the world around darkened even further, and if it hadn't been for the sound of Jennifer's scream of anguish, he might have let himself fall the rest of the way to the ground.

Instead, he left his mounted position so his guy could sit up. Then he pushed in under the guy's guard to shoot into a guillotine choke. He locked it in and stepped back to throw his hips into it, and the guy had no leverage to counter. A few seconds later with one last jerk, Mark heard something in the guy's neck tear, and he dropped the body to tumble down the concrete pile to splash into the cove.

While he caught his breath, he had to try two times to get his leg to work so he could crawl to Jennifer's side. He whistled a song under his breath, and he smiled when he finally recognized it.

He shivered as he reached her side. He was freezing. She couldn't have been any better off. She was nearly naked, and *he* had shoes. He talked to her to distract her as he led her to the base of a tree offering meager shelter from the rain. Nonsense that popped into his mind. Anecdotes and memories.

He sat next to her and rubbed his knee to get it going again. Usually, when it was done, that was it. Pain meds and rest. Maybe it would be ready the next day. Most times, not. Right now, he needed it.

"There was an explosion on the cruiser I was stationed on. I think I mentioned earlier. The *Northville*? Anyway, one of my — one of the guys that worked for the weapons officers. He had some mental issue that went undiagnosed for too long. Thoughts of self-harm and ... well, yeah."

He didn't want to tell her any of his story, but the way she stared at him — like she was lost, and his words were what she was using to find her way back. He decided to keep going, but he looked away.

"Anyway, he kinda slipped through the cracks. Like a lot of us, I guess."

Mark pushed out from under the leaves. He went to his guy's body first. He worked the shirt off. It was soaked. Probably had a lot of blood in it too. It wouldn't keep him warm, but it would protect his skin from collecting more scratches and cuts.

He felt around for ammo pouches. Found two on the guy's belt. Slid them off before feeling in the sand for the dropped weapon. He found it under an edge of concrete that stabbed into his knuckles. He stuck them in his mouth with a hiss of pain as he carried everything to pile it at Jennifer's feet.

Instead of staring at him, she stared into space until he clapped his hands, then her gaze focused on his face.

"He had been hurting for a while, but nobody saw it," he continued. "It's tough to know what to do for people like that. If it's outside your sphere of experience or whatever, you just dismiss it."

"Is that what you did?" she asked.

Mark sighed as he turned away. Every step on his bad leg sent burning fire up into his side. His knee felt like hot mush filled with rusty nails.

Mark eased down next to the other guy. He looked away from the pulp of his face to feel for ammo pouches and any weapons. One belt, four pouches, a KA-BAR knife in a black canvas sheath, and the gun Jennifer had used to kill him.

He brought it all back to add to the pile. This time, she watched him the entire time.

"Yes," he said. "That's exactly what I did. And when it came time for him to end his personal suffering, he chose to blow up the ammo stores on the boat."

Mark ducked back into the rain a third time. It looked like the guy he had killed had the smaller feet of the two, so he worked his boots off. He dragged them back to the tree and sat down next to her.

He busied himself with loosening the laces. Adjusting the size of the belts. He pulled her up onto her knees to reach around her to put the belt on her waist. Picked the gun up and cleared it before dropping it into the holster.

Then he leaned back and forced a smile. "You look ridiculous."

Her mouth twitched in a smile. Then she looked at the ground. "How did it happen?"

Mark put his own belt on. Holstered the pistol. He wished the guy he had killed had a bigger chest so he could close the shirt, but at least his back was protected.

"I figured out what was happening a little too late. I tried to help, but the damage was done. Almost lost my leg. Forced to retire. Nightmares for years..." Mark sighed and rubbed both hands over his face. "But I was one of the lucky ones, so they say." He pointed over his shoulder. "Doesn't feel very fucking lucky to me."

Jennifer sat back down and hugged her knees to her chest. "I'm sorry."

Mark laughed. "For what?"

"About what happened to you."

Mark bit back his annoyance. "How about being sorry for your husband trying to kill me?"

He immediately regretted it, but she nodded.

"I'm sorry for that too."

"Look. We gotta get out of here, okay?"

She shrugged.

"It looks like the power is out."

"Then what are those lights?"

"Marker lights for the airstrips on a backup generator. We're technically on base right now."

"Is there anybody who can help us?"

"Maybe. But Reg said he was military. Was he lying?"

Jennifer shook her head.

"Then he can get through the gates. He might already be on his way."

"Okay."

"Okay what?"

"Okay, we have to go."

Mark didn't like that she responded like a zombie. He

also didn't like how he felt responsible for her for some reason. It wasn't because she was pretty ... though she certainly was. More now with her ponytail pulled out and plastered to her head as the rain dripped down her neck and shoulders.

Her doe eyes looking up at him for guidance.

He was such a sucker.

"*I'm* sorry," he said.

She drew back in confusion. "For what?"

"Just in general, you know?"

"No, I don't."

He had to admit that he didn't either. "Look, we can't go by sea. My boat is toast. We have to go inland. Maybe find a car or an MP. Flag somebody down. Get help, right?"

"Right." She shivered as she looked out at the sky from under the leaves.

She reminded him of something. The way she sat there staring. A memory right at the edge of his awareness. When he suddenly realized who it was she reminded him of, he tried to push the memory back down, but it was too late.

Gerry Disantis. Everybody called him GD, and he was one of the best friends Mark had ever had. A man down for any adventure, no matter how small or how overblown and ill-advised.

Riding their bicycles through the Keys to stop to catch lobsters every night, living two in a tent and spacing out the rest stops to match with a brewery or a distillery, or a bar with a good selection of tequila.

Panning for gold in Alaska. Buying a used RV sight unseen in Florida and driving it over two thousand miles to Las Vegas so they could get kicked out of the Dry Heart Casino for counting cards. Buying a thousand dollars' worth of supplies from The Dollar Tree to cook hotdogs at the San Benito Pier for the homeless people living on the beach.

GD had made a million dollars in various schemes and businesses in the first year they had known each other, and he couldn't understand why Mark didn't want to do any of them with him. "It's free money," he had said. "You just have to do the work."

It wasn't the work Mark didn't care for. It was the cycle of need that scared him away. GD was never satisfied. He never celebrated a win, instead just looking for the next thing to beat.

GD tried to get him to churn credit cards for the travel points. He had complicated spreadsheets with payments schedules and totals. Cycling through different cards depending on where they were going and what they were buying. Mark got the concept, especially when GD paid for several trips with nothing but points, but he just couldn't grasp the mechanics.

When GD finally found a girlfriend, Mark had breathed a silent sigh of relief. He loved him like a brother, but a little GD went a long way. He couldn't keep up with how quickly his mind moved from one idea to another.

Like many friends after a woman gets involved, Mark and GD grew apart. It wasn't a bad thing, just a thing that happened. Mark was happy for his friend's new life, and he celebrated it whenever they got together. When they announced their wedding, GD paid for him and a bunch of their mutual friends to come to Hawaii where they blessed the happy couple.

The same weekend GD found a lump in his left testicle.

It was months later when Mark found out. GD showed up thin and pale. The doctors had told him there was no hope for him. Chemo, radiation, and removing the testicle hadn't been enough. It had already started to spread. They stopped treatment, and GD rented a van to drive to Florida to see his friend one last time. And he was alone. Sheila had left him shortly after the Hawaii party when he had gone to the doctor for the initial diagnosis.

"I don't blame her," GD said. "I wouldn't want anyone to live through something like that."

Mark had forced a confused smile. "Then why make *me* do it?"

Seeing his friend laugh had made it easier to watch him die.

One night, they had sat in front of a fire over a bottle of Jameson. Dunking Fig Newtons into the whiskey between puffs on their Padron 64's. In spite of the heat rolling from the flames, GD nearly shivered inside the Mexican blanket wrapped around his shoulder. "I gave all my money away," he said.

"Yeah?"

"You have your retirement, so I figured you didn't need it."

"That's right."

GD waited, but when Mark said nothing else, he blew a dramatic sigh. "Don't you want to know who gets it?"

"If you wanna tell me, sure."

"Of *course*, I want to tell you. Why are you the way you are?"

Mark shrugged and dunked another Fig Newton.

"Fine, I gave it all to Nugget."

Mark snorted whiskey into his nose. He bent to the side to cough out the half-chewed cookie into the sand. He finally caught his breath and sat up to wipe the tears from his eyes. "Her fucking *cat*?"

"Technically, he's *my* cat. We weren't ever actually married. She just took him."

"How much does he get?"

"Two-point-five million."

Mark closed his eyes. He knew it was just a gesture. One last defiance before GD died. When he opened his eyes, GD looked wistfully at the gathering clouds.

"I wish it would hold off just a couple more days."

"What, the storm?"

"Yeah. But it's okay. So what if it storms for the last few days I'm alive? I remember what the sun looks like. I might miss it, but I ain't gonna bitch and moan for the rest of my life."

That's how Jennifer looked at the clouds. Like it was never going to end, and she'd never see the sky again.

"How long is it supposed to last?" she asked.

"The news said just for a few hours."

He didn't know if the truth had been the right answer, but it was better than what he had wanted to say.

He'd almost said, "The rest of my life."

He wasn't enjoying himself anymore.

Chapter Sixteen

When Mark grabbed her ankle, she let him pull her leg out straight. When she saw him pull one of the boots over, she almost drew her leg back up, but she looked down at the glistening rocks covering the ground.

She turned her head away and let him put the boots of a dead man on her feet.

They were too big, but he cinched the tops tight around her ankles and lower calves. They would keep her feet from getting cut to ribbons.

"Let's go before another crocodile comes by for a snack," Mark said. "And there are alligators too, so…"

She knew he was joking, but her body wasn't so sure. She was on her feet and clinging to him before he was done talking.

He staggered back with a surprised smile. She was thankful it was too dark to see her embarrassment. She peeled herself away and grabbed the pistol out of the holster that hung too low. Checked the magazine and chamber out of habit before switching the safety off and resting her finger along the trigger guard.

She looked up to catch Mark staring at her. "What?"

"I don't know. You think you'll get a divorce when this is over?"

That was what he wanted to ask?

"If I don't kill him first," she snarled.

"Well, if you're not through with all men by then, look me up."

She barked laughter with an unbelieving shake of her head. "My rebound boyfriend is gonna be the guy that helped me kill him? I don't think so."

Mark shrugged, but the considering expression stayed on his face. "Just keep an open mind."

Was he serious? At a time like this?

She thought about the dead man she was going to leave behind. Johnson. Then Anderson, the man Mark had killed. Finally, she thought about Mark's story. How he was held hostage by his own guilt. He lived in the prison of his past, same as she'd been living trapped in an abusive marriage.

She pointed her gun into the darkness. "Lead the way."

His smile became smug as he turned and hunched his shoulders against the rain. She spent too much time trying to figure out why he looked that way instead of watching for danger. Her boots squelched with every step, but there didn't seem to be any bad rubbing. The image of Johnson's dying face flashed into her mind, but she pushed it down to focus on the memory of Mark's smile instead.

After a few minutes, the ground changed from gritty sand to cracked asphalt, and the trees and bushes thinned out. A loud whining in the distance had replaced the constant sound of the wind.

She stumbled to a halt. "Hey, the rain stopped."

She had walked all the way from the beach in a daze

thinking about a man. A *stranger* with a nice smile … who had saved her life.

"Yeah," Mark said. "But the clouds still look pretty pissed."

He was right. They looked like the billowing smoke from a gasoline explosion spreading across the sky, but the hint of light at the horizon promised an end to the storms altogether.

A few more yards, and they were out in the open on the asphalt and concrete of the airstrip itself. She tripped on a glowing reflector, nearly dropping to her knees.

"You okay?" Mark whispered.

She did too. "Yeah. Just wondering where we're going."

He moved to her shoulder and pointed. She squinted at a small pale blob next to a large black blob.

"Okay?" she said.

"It's a base vehicle."

Now that she knew what she was looking at, she could tell it was a white SUV of some kind. "Are we going to steal it?"

"Maybe. I'm sure the keys are in it — they normally are — but first we might just see if there are any clothes in it. Then find whoever drove it here and maybe get some help."

She holstered her gun. "Who drove it?"

"No idea, but nobody's in it. They're probably in the generator house."

That was the dark blob, then. A building with a gener-ator in it. "Is that's what making that whining sound? Keeping the landing lights on?"

Mark crouched down next to the passenger door. "Yeah, but those are just warning lights to show any passing aircraft the location of towers and anything else

NAS doesn't want lost in the night. It probably runs on natural gas or propane. I'm not sure."

He opened the door and shielded his eyes against the glare of the dome light. He looked around the interior before pushing his thumb against the door switch to shut the light off.

Jennifer hadn't thought to look away. Now all she saw was a lingering bright spot in the shape of the door's outline. Mark pressed fabric into her hand.

"Put this on," he said.

It was the slick nylon of a windbreaker, dark with bright orange markings on the sleeves. She shrugged into it with a soft moan, then zipped it up and shoved her hands into the pockets. It smelled like vanilla cookies. "Did you see any food in there?"

"Nope. No keys, either."

"So, we go inside?"

He nodded and eased the door shut. "I thought we'd have to anyway. I was kinda hoping just to fuck off to the marina to make a few phone calls from my houseboat."

He stood up and pulled her toward the outbuilding. She resisted the urge to snatch her arm from his grip. When they had taken a few steps, he let her go. He hadn't been trying to control her, just guide her. He wasn't treating her like a fragile flower.

It felt like courtesy. She wasn't used to that.

A gray cinder block building with a gray metal door formed out of the shadows. Mark holstered his weapon and looked back at her with his hand hovering above the handle.

She suppressed a shiver. "What?"

"Your husband could have had enough time to report us. To who knows who, saying who knows what. I don't know what's in there."

She took a half step back. "You're leaving it up to me?"

"No, just letting you know what I'm thinking."

"Okay, what else are you thinking?"

"I'm thinking we have to weigh the two big options. Do we find a cop or an MP and trust that our voices will be heard, our word against his? Or do we fight? Can your husband reach us in custody? Can he track us? Do you know anybody who can help? Anything?"

She crossed her arms and thought about his questions. "I don't know what he eventually wants. I know right now, he needs me dead. I don't think he'll be satisfied with anything else, and with me gone, my parents are a target. Especially if they don't believe him."

"Will they?"

She wanted to say *no*, but the way Don treated him — like the son he always wanted but never had … And Janet fawned over him like *she* was the one to marry him. She suddenly wasn't so sure.

"I don't know, but St. James Protection has a lot of resources. Weapons, surveillance gear, and personnel. He can probably easily track us. He's been moving in men loyal to him for months. Lots of jobs for his Army buddies."

Mark held up his hand. "Okay. So we do both."

"What do you mean?"

"Whoever's in there, we'll tell our story to 'em, then take their keys. Then we'll stop your husband."

She nodded, but asked, "Why won't you use his name?"

"Because he tried to kill me. And I don't like the way he treated you."

He broke eye contact like the admission embarrassed him. Instead of replying, she pushed his hand down on the doorknob and stepped back.

Fresh rain fell to ring off the metal, its sizzle rising with the wind to cover the whine of the generator.

With a final nod, Mark opened the door and rushed inside with his other hand held above his pistol.

She ducked to use him as cover and followed him inside.

Chapter Seventeen

The whine became a roar as they stepped inside. The bright light dazzled his eyes, but Mark could still see the interior through his squinted eyelids.

A figure squatted in front of a generator on the back wall. The green metal cover leaned against the wall, and the figure curled in to connect leads from an ohm meter into some rusty lugs inside the frame. Large yellow earmuffs rested against his head. They were half covered by long curly hair plastered to his head. A dark blue jacket with orange letters — CIVILIAN — down the sleeves that matched the one he'd given Jennifer.

A civilian contractor out to check the generator's output.

Mark pulled his gun and leaned forward to tap the barrel on the earmuff head strap.

The figure whipped around in panic. The meter flew into the wall. The sugar cookie he had been stuffing into his mouth crumbled against his chin, spilling crumbs down his shirt. His wispy mustache and goatee were covered in yellow dust.

Mark aimed his pistol at the guy's face.

"The fuck are *you*?" Mark shouted.

The guy slowly lifted his hands, his gaze fixed on the gun barrel. He took a deep breath. "I'm Brad, man!"

"What are you doing here?"

"What?"

Mark edged closer. "What are you *doing*?"

Brad cupped his hands behind his earmuffs. "What!"

Mark looked at the control panel on the generator. A big red button under the main power switch. He slapped it, and the generator wound down like a slowing train.

"Hey, don't do that!" Brad screamed. In the sudden silence, his voice cracked like he was going through puberty. He realized how loud he had been. Slid his earmuffs back and took a deep breath.

"Sorry," he said. Just above a whisper. "But you shouldn't have done that."

Jennifer stepped around to look up at Mark. "I kind of believe him."

Mark was relieved that she seemed to have warmed up after her near comatose state out under the mangroves.

She looked down at the floor, and her eyes widened with excitement as she squealed. "Ooh!"

Brad flinched away when she dropped down into a squat next to him. His face went from concerned to offended when she stood up, holding a clear plastic container full of cookies. She took a dramatic smell before lifting one out. "Some of them have little M&M's in them."

She took a bite and closed her eyes in pleasure. If it wasn't for Brad held at gunpoint on the floor in front of him, Mark would have watched her eat the whole cookie.

Mark held his hand up to get Brad's attention again. "What are you doing here?"

"Just checking the gennie, man. I was on call for the storm. Captain Drummond put me in the rotation."

"You're a civilian?"

"That's right. I couldn't get in. I got IBS."

Mark lifted his gun. "Stand up, Brad."

Brad used a metal conduit to help himself off the floor. "You gonna eat all my cookies?"

Jennifer stopped with another cookie in front of her lips. "You have any other food?"

"No."

"Then, *maybe*."

He seemed more upset about it than the gun.

"Focus, Brad," Mark said. "Look at me."

Brad nodded, but when he looked back, Mark could tell his heart wasn't in it.

"I need your keys, okay?"

"To what?"

"Your mom's house. The fuck you think? The base vehicle outside."

"No way. I signed it out. It's my ass if anything happens to it."

Jennifer pointed at him with the last bite of her cookie. "It's your ass if you don't listen. You may notice, he has a gun pointed at your face."

Brad swallowed. "Oh, I notice."

"Good," Mark said. "The keys."

Brad sighed. He dug into his pocket and handed Mark a ring of keys hanging from a keychain that looked like a tiny container of french fries. "That's also hand sanitizer."

Mark handed the keys to Jennifer. "Good to know. Now, listen to me. I need you to tell them a story when they come to see what you fucked up."

Brad threw his arms up. "Man, I didn't do anything. It was *you*."

Jennifer closed the cookie container and held it out. "I saved you a couple."

Brad's face lit with excitement. "Hey, thanks!"

Mark stepped back and pinched the bridge of his nose. "Can we focus?"

Jennifer smiled. "Sorry."

"That's why I turned it off. So someone would notice and come out here. You got a phone?"

"The network's down."

"That's not what I asked, Brad."

Brad wilted. "Yeah, I got a phone."

"Would you give it to her, please?"

"Yeah."

"Sorry," Jennifer whispered.

Brad smiled at her from under his brow. "It's okay."

"That's nice," Mark said.

Jennifer looked at the screen. "What's your pin?"

"Eight three seven two."

Jennifer entered it, then her shoulder sagged as she frowned. "He's right. No signal."

"Perfect," Mark said. He pointed at a tool bag by Brad's feet. "That yours?"

"Yeah?"

"Any zip ties in there?"

"Yeah."

"Good. We're gonna tie you to one of these pipes here, and when they come to check on the generator, tell them what's up."

"But I don't know what's up," Brad whined.

Jennifer stepped forward and put her hand on Brad's shoulder. He looked at her like she was an angel. Mark was starting to feel the same way.

"My husband is trying to kill us," she said.

She pushed him down until he was sitting on his knees.

She took the cookies from him and set them on the floor within his reach.

"He sent men after us that we had to kill after they blew up this man's boat. I'm afraid he might go after my parents next."

"Oh no," Brad said, staring at her lips.

Jennifer slung the tool bag toward Mark. He dropped down to dig through it with one hand. The zip ties were right on top, next to a roll of electrical tape.

"We're afraid that if we get caught by the authorities, he might have men there waiting for us, and it won't matter what the truth is."

"That sucks."

Mark wasn't sure if Brad was dumb as paint or just in shock. He was an electrical contractor, so he had *some* kind of mind. Mark imagined how insane it would be to go out in a storm to check on a military generator only to have somebody run in pointing a gun.

"Can you remember all that, Brad?"

He swallowed and nodded. "No."

Mark handed her two zip ties. She only took one. "We'll just do his left hand so he can still eat his cookies."

Maybe she *was* an angel.

Mark waited until the hand was secured before putting his gun away. "I don't think it will matter. As long as they know that we shut the generator off on purpose to get somebody out here, the other details are just filler."

"Right," Brad said. "Why would you *want* somebody coming after you if you were guilty, right?"

Jennifer grinned. "Exactly."

"He can probably get out of that," Mark said.

She stood, then looked down at Brad. "We're leaving now. Just finish your cookies before you try to break that thing, okay?"

Brad smiled with a shrug. "Sure."

She looked back at Mark. "Good?"

Mark lifted the french fry sanitizer and found the black plastic key fobs that cars were using nowadays. He held it up for Brad to see. "This it?"

Brad tore his attention away from his cookie. "Yeah."

Mark pulled Jennifer to the door, but when he opened it, stinging rain blew into his eyes. He shielded his face and jogged to the driver's side. He jumped in, and Jennifer was only a second behind him. She settled in as he started the SUV.

"Where are we going?" she asked.

"This air strip is connected to the beach next to Sediment Key. Only military has access, and they check IDs at the entrance, but not for anybody *leaving*, especially in a base vehicle. Then it's just a couple blocks to the marina. *They* don't check ID's."

"So, Reg and his men could get in here?"

"Yeah, but how would they know where to look?"

"I guess."

The uncertainty in her voice made him want to pat her arm and tell her it was going to be alright, but he resisted.

He felt sorry for Brad, and for the way Jennifer had dazzled him. He glanced over at her, but with nothing but dash lights, it was hard to see her.

He wondered what she saw when she looked at him.

Chapter Eighteen

Hayes sat behind the wheel of Reg's Jeep. After dropping Reg off back at the hotel, it was a quick trip to the entrance of the Sediment Key beach. According to Jennifer's tracking dot, she was still on foot, moving across an airstrip almost a mile in from the cove.

A break in the weather had seemed promising, but by the time they got in line at the gate, it had started raining again. He looked over at Harris sitting in the passenger seat, bent over a small monitor. His red hair looked painted on.

"She still moving?" Hayes asked.

Harris shook his head. "Nah, it looks like she stopped. Right on the strip. Say, two miles off the beach."

Lewis, one of the men in the backseat, leaned forward over the center console to look at the red dot on the screen. His dark skin made his teeth shine when he talked. "What for?"

Harris snorted laughter. "How should I know? Maybe she's taking a piss."

Hayes glanced up in the rearview mirror. There was

nobody else behind him. He looked back out the windshield to see the old-timer with a RETIRED NAVY trucker hat and a yellow safety vest shuffle out to the car in front of them.

A big pantomime telling them the beach was closed because of the storm, then the old-timer pointed to a turnaround where he had sent the other cars. Hayes slammed his hand on the wheel.

"What?" Lewis said.

Hayes sighed. "We might have to do some work here."

Hayes had nearly been court-martialed. Technically, not his fault, but when you fuck the base commander's wife, the brass doesn't see it that way. The only thing that saved him was that the couple had been in the middle of a divorce after a long separation.

He'd left the Army earlier than he wanted to, but he still had friends — like Reg and the rest of his unit — and he used his veteran status for everything from discounts at cigar stores … to getting onto beaches in Key West that only servicemembers could access.

When the old-timer finished turning the car in front of them around, Hayes pulled up next to the sliding glass door in the brick guard shack and rolled his window down an inch. Rain sputtered in through the crack.

The Navy retiree shuffled out with an apologetic grin. "Been telling 'em all. The beach is shut down until the storm passes."

"What about people already there?" Hayes shouted.

The old man shrugged. "Got patrol out keeping them out of the water. Who would want to be out there in weather like this anyway?"

Hayes smiled with a nod. "I understand. Do I turn around just ahead, then?"

"That's right."

"Thank you, sir. And what's your name?"

"Portis. Frank Portis."

Hayes looked up into the rearview to catch Lewis' eye. He nodded as he thumbed the door lock switch. Lewis nodded back and stepped into the rain to follow Frank Portis into the little shack.

The old man turned in surprise, but Lewis was already swinging. His fist caught the old man dead in the face, sending him crashing back with his arms straight out to either side. Blood flew up from his crushed nose in an arc that carried almost all the way to the ceiling. His hat flew off like a tossed Frisbee.

Lewis jumped forward as Frank fell. He dumped the old man over and removed his reflective vest. He donned it with a roll of his shoulders before dropping down to put his knee on the back of Frank's neck.

He put his silenced pistol to the old man's head and squeezed the trigger twice. There was less blood than Hayes expected. Maybe the punch and the fall had already killed him.

Lewis scooped up the hat while he kicked the body under the shelf next to the door to get it out of sight. He pulled the hat down and stepped out into the rain.

Hayes rolled his window all the way down. Fuck Reg's interior. It was a Jeep, right? It was supposed to be able to get wet. "Sit out here for a few minutes until you're good and wet, so it looks like you been helping a long line of cars."

Lewis nodded. "Roger that."

"Phones are still out, so use the encoded channel."

It had less range, but nobody could listen in.

"She's moving again," Harris shouted.

Hayes glanced over to see the red dot creeping across the screen.

"Looks like she ain't walking anymore," Harris said.

"We'll contact you if they get past us, but this is the only way in by vehicle. Watch for 'em."

Lewis stepped back with a nod. "Will do."

Hayes rolled the window up and hit the gas. They lurched away from the entrance and down the lane toward the beach. Lightning lit the area into an instant of daylight. The thunder was right on top of it.

Cox, the other man in the back seat, clapped his hands. His buck-toothed grin looked like the opening to a tunnel. "Damn boys, she's right on top of us now."

"Nope," Harris said. He pointed at the screen. "We're right on top of *her*."

Hayes thought that wasn't a bad place to be.

Chapter Nineteen

Jennifer adjusted the vent to blow in her face. Then she closed it in frustration. It would be a minute or two before the air coming from the blower warmed up.

She zipped the windbreaker up to her chin, but it wasn't doing it. She needed something more. She looked over at Mark and suddenly felt selfish. He didn't even have a shirt on.

She hit the safety switch on her pistol before putting it back in the holster. Mark's nod of approval from the corner of her eye infuriated her. She bit back her rising indignation. Of *course* a woman could do things, fight and handle weapons…

Then she remembered how she had let Reg dictate how she dressed. How he treated her in private. It wasn't fair to be judged under any circumstances, but she never would have worn so little if Reg hadn't forced it. It had just become easier to cave to his demands than face the fight later. And that had been the Jennifer that Mark had met first, the one who allowed herself to be Reg's plaything.

Fine. Mark seemed okay, but she was still cold. She

unbuckled her belt and turned around to lean into the back seat. Without headlights or dome lights, her eyes were getting used to the dark, but she still couldn't see anything but dark shapes.

Her fingers dug through the backseat. The crinkle of candy bar wrappers. A backpack's canvas strap. Soft fabric in the shape of a hoodie.

She turned back in her seat with a low cry of victory. She spread the hoodie out and tipped it into the dim light filtering through the clouds and rain. It was gray with red lettering — *SLOPPY JOE'S*. A matching caricature of Hemingway over the left breast.

Mark cursed under his breath.

Jennifer dropped the hoodie into her lap to look at his face. He split his gaze between his rear-view window and the rocky beach in front of them. She looked over her shoulder but saw nothing but rain.

"What is it?" she asked.

"I don't know. I thought I saw headlights out there, kinda cutting the angle off between here and where we pick up the road, but whoever it was either shut them off or turned away."

Visibility was near zero outside, and she didn't know what to look for except another light. She left it to Mark as she struggled out of the windbreaker. It stuck to every inch of her skin, and there didn't seem to be enough room for her to maneuver her arms straight behind her.

She had to put her forehead on the dash before she had the space to peel the wet jacket off. She balled it up with a sigh of relief and tossed it in the back seat. "I didn't think it would fit you," she said.

"What wouldn't fit?"

"The windbreaker. Brad was a little soggy, but he was still smaller than you."

"I'm fine."

"That's what men *always* say."

"You sound like my therapist."

"She must be good at her job."

The corner of his mouth twitched in a smile. "What makes you think she's a woman?"

Jennifer ran her arms into the sleeves of the hoodie. "Because her advice sounded very sensible."

"Men aren't sensible?"

She paused to contemplate the tone of his voice. This would have been a delicate subject if she had been talking to Reg. Anything that highlighted gender differences — especially if men came out looking bad — made Reg step onto his soapbox. A lecture about how men built the world, followed by how it was proven that women were happier with lives spent nurturing as opposed to pursuing a profession. Then, down the rabbit hole of conservative values and how the youth of today are all going to their own private hell. She was just so tired of it.

But Mark's amusement felt genuine. He was playful instead of offended. It was like ... he was flirting?

"Oh, men are good for *some* things," she said.

He laughed like he didn't believe her. "Name one."

"Wait a minute, whose side are you on?"

"Oh, yeah. *I'm* a man. Well, we're good at pushing our emotions down."

"Barbeque."

"That's right. And drinking beer."

"Fishing."

"Well, *some* of us. At least, that's what we brag about."

"Reg brags about everything."

"Then what's *he* really good at?"

"Being an asshole."

"Shooting up my boat."

"Making me feel like shit."

She looked up to see his easy grin had been replaced by sympathy. It was almost as bad as seeing Reg's smug smile as he pointed at the ceiling.

To keep from seeing it — and to hide the hurt on her own face — she pulled the hoodie over her head to get it the rest of the way on.

"Shit!" Mark shouted. "Hang on!"

How? She was swallowed by the hoodie.

She threw her right hand out to feel for the handle on the door while her left hand clawed and pulled at the hoodie to get her head through the neck hole. She froze at the sound of an approaching engine.

The clash of metal on metal, and the base vehicle jumped toward the water, bouncing her sideways over the center console into Mark's shoulder. Her head popped out of the hoodie, and the world tilted sideways, throwing her back into her own seat.

Her temple cracked off the window in a blazing daze of white light and pain.

The crash of another impact rode over the splash of water that slammed her flat against her door. Gravity told her the side of the SUV was now down. Somebody had hit them into the water.

She sat up, and the window creaked under her weight. Cold water splattered against her hips and up the small of her back. It spilled over the tops of her boots to soak her feet.

Another screech of metal, and the SUV lurched farther out to sea. The seat cushion pressing into her face was still warm from where she had just been sitting in it.

She got her feet underneath her to stand up, and her boots crunched through the glass to sink into sand. A deflated airbag flopped against her hip.

The vehicle settled into the sound of the rain, and she rose up to listen, but she bumped into Mark's side. He hung above her from his seatbelt, fighting to get his own airbag out of his face.

He growled in frustration.

Gunfire erupted outside. She crouched back down and covered her head as bullets thunked into the undercarriage. She thought about all the training she had finished. Unarmed self-defense. Active shooter. SWAT. Sending hate down range in every set of circumstances her instructors could come up with.

Not one had included being shot at in a vehicle on its side as it slid into the ocean.

The water was now up to her waist. She pulled her pistol and held it ready, aimed into the back cushion of her seat so it wasn't pointed at Mark. "Is that him?"

She felt something trickle down the side of her face. She hoped it wasn't blood.

"How do I know?" he shouted.

"I don't know. Maybe you looked out the window before he hit us."

"I mean, it looked like the same Jeep. The guy with the thyroid problem."

"Then it was him."

"Or somebody else driving *his* vehicle."

Probably Hayes.

More gunfire, and she hunkered down.

"Fuck this," Mark said.

He laid his seat back all the way and opened his seatbelt. He caught himself from crashing down on her, but he still kneed her in the side of the head.

"Jesus Christ!" she squealed.

"Sorry."

He worked his way into the back seat so he was

standing on the rear door. She brushed the airbag out of the way and stood up as much as she could. The water crept over the center console. "I hate that thing," she said.

Mark pulled his gun and pressed into the ceiling. "What thing?"

"His stupid Jeep. I had one, but as soon as he got the Napoleon Edition, I sold it. Bought a Dodge Ram instead, and he was pissed because mine was bigger than his."

Mark's surprised laughter made her grin, but more shots fired made her bite back her own laughter. She looked at him over the side of her seat. "What are we gonna do?"

"That's a good question."

"Thank you."

Mark pushed off the ceiling. "Let's get the fuck outta here."

She could tell he wasn't sure how they were going to do it. No reassurances or pep talks. Just a call to action. Reg would have talked it to death until the bullets hit the gas tank and they exploded. "Wait a minute. Can this thing blow up?"

"See?" Mark said. "Another good question."

Chapter Twenty

Mark found it unlikely that anyone could have found them so quickly. Then again, anybody familiar with the area might have gotten lucky. "That's pretty fucking lucky, though."

"What is?"

He waved the bitter dust from the deployed airbags away from his face. The water lapped at his belly button. "I'll have to find out later."

"Sounds good to me."

He smiled as another round of gunfire lit into the bottom of their SUV. It sounded like a semi-automatic rifle. He knew the bottoms of the base vehicles were armored, but that was still a lot of power. It only took a hole in the gas tank to let the vapor escape. Then a spark. Then … the thought of an explosion made his throat tighten. He swallowed and moved into the cargo area.

He reached back for Jennifer. "Climb on back here."

When he turned to see her already scampering over the seat to join him, he almost applauded. When he saw her protecting the pistol from the rising water, he bit back a whistle of appreciation. There was more to this woman than anybody could possibly know, because they just weren't seeing her.

He had no idea if that last part was actually true, but he believed it.

Even with her face covered in blood and her hair tangled and matted to the side of her head, he couldn't stop looking at her. She planted her feet and looked up. "What?"

He blinked and looked away. "I think I have a plan."

"Oh yeah? Tell me more."

"I'm gonna jump out shooting."

"That's it?"

"Well, there's no real strategy. Just get out there and start blasting. I mean, we're dead if we stay."

"The hell, you say."

He smiled to himself. There was *so* much more.

"Just get right up behind me."

More bullets hit the undercarriage, and he dropped down to put his chin level with the water. They must have stopped sliding down into the ocean. The water was no longer rising.

"I'm gonna kick out the back glass. Fire blind around the corner while you come out behind me."

"Then what? I cover you so you can get around to the other side?"

"No. Just get out there and swim for it."

"What?"

"You're in good shape. Water's not *too* cold. Get out there and swim along the coast."

"While you what? Get killed to give me time?"

"If that's what happens, yes. Look, we have to do it

anyway, or else they'll come out here to check on us. They might even be on their way right now."

She shrugged. "Fine."

He stared at the resolve on her face. It wasn't the first time he had been lied to by a woman. She intended to stay and fight with him.

It didn't matter. He knew the current would take her out anyway. "Fine," he said.

He worked his body into position, so that his back was braced against the rear seats, then he lifted his knees up to put his feet against the back glass. He kicked with everything he had, and the window became a web of cracks, but it barely gave way.

His knee screamed, and jagged agony raced up his leg. He wasn't sure he had another kick in him, but he drew his legs up again. Before he had the chance to go again, a shadow appeared outside. He was too late.

Jennifer's pistol came into view, and he turned his head away as she opened fire. When she finished dumping the whole mag into the glass, there was nothing left but tattered shards hanging from the edges.

Water pushed against him, and the shadow — now clearly a man holding an assault rifle — staggered back to fall on his ass with blood flowing from his mouth.

Through the ugly ringing now in his ears, Mark heard Jennifer's scream of triumph as she released the expended magazine, fished a fresh one out of the pouch on her belt, and drove it in with a practiced hand. The slide racked home, and she grinned at him with manic glee.

Bullets struck the rear of the SUV and splattered into the water between them, the injured man scrambling desperately through the waves back to shore.

Mark dropped his feet, and even with the water taking

up some of his weight, his knee buckled, grinding as it gave way. He braced against the window frame, driving his good leg straight to keep him upright. Broken glass dug into his shoulder and upper arm.

He transferred the pistol to his left hand and leaned out to aim around the top of the window. "*Go!*" he shouted.

He laid down steady fire as she waded out into the receding waves. They pulled her out and away from the SUV just like he'd thought they would, but when he pulled back in to reload, Jennifer splashed away from the bumper to dump her second mag.

He bit back a curse and jumped to move into the space between her and the SUV. As her empty magazine dropped into the water, he took fire, and she dodged back behind him. Now, when he moved to stand behind the roof of the SUV, they'd both be protected.

But a car was actually poor cover. Bullets often tended to find their way through all that metal. Thankfully, the skid plates on the bottom were stopping most of them.

Return fire from the shore made him duck into the water to put his back against the roof. Jennifer stood next to him, and the incoming waves drove her into the metal. "Why aren't you out there getting away?" he hissed.

"I can't swim."

"Fucking *what?*"

"I'm kidding. I'm just not leaving without you."

"Why the fuck not?"

She pushed her face up into his. "Because I'm not letting you die for me. One of them is already down. They're gonna regroup. Now's our chance to get out there."

Mark seethed as he drew away from her. Why was it so important that she get away without him? He swiped rain away from his eyes, but he didn't answer. He didn't know what to say.

"Besides, I don't know the area. You do. You wanna save me so bad, *save* me. But do it *with* me."

He slotted his pistol back into the holster. He hoped the wet velcro would hold.

Another round of gunfire popped into the SUV. When she didn't flinch, he grabbed her face in his hands. "You better make it, because I need to know more about you."

She smiled and pulled his hands away. "I'll see what I can do."

The smell of gas hit like a wet towel across his face. He grabbed her into an embrace and dug his feet into the sand. She squawked against his chest, but he pushed off before she could get away. Like he was trying to suplex her over the ocean, he spun her into an arc that slammed her into the water underneath him.

His ears still rang from the shots inside the SUV, but he heard the gunfire from shore just fine. Then the roar of the water rushing past his ears.

Every kick away from shore sent daggers from his knee into his thigh. A sickening burn that felt like it would consume his entire leg.

Jennifer held on and kicked along with him, but her knees slapped into his balls with every stroke.

Still, he swam.

Up for a quick breath, and he looked back at the muzzle flashes lighting the underside of the mangrove leaves. Her desperate breath next to him, and he put them back under.

The SUV exploded with a crunching rumble that slammed into his guts like the force of hitting the bottom of a hill in a racecar. A small sun burned behind them.

Mark came up sputtering into burning air. Fiery debris

sprinkling around him. He heard someone shout his name. Saw the stairwell open in front of him, smoke billowing out with the sounds of his men dying below deck.

He dove in to save them — just *one*, please God — but all his hands found was sand.

Chapter Twenty-One

Mark let go of her, and the current pulled her away. The soaked hoodie was an anchor, but the gun was solid in her hand. Something to grab on to, even if it wasn't keeping her afloat.

She thrashed around, but her movements weren't effective. Nothing could keep her from being swept out deeper. Why would Mark have wanted her to swim out here by herself?

When her boots hit a bank of broken concrete, she suddenly got it. She planted her feet on the uneven surface and looked away from the rolling flames of the destroyed vehicle. Buoys stretched out along the shore, marking the location of the man-made barrier. She could pretty much walk to safety.

She squinted against the glare and looked back. One figure hunched over in front of the flames. Another shadow man with his arm thrown over the first's shoulder. Voices floating to her on the wind. No words, just panic.

Again, she remembered the family pool. Don shouting at her to save him as he pretended to drown. He had put her in a box shaped like what he thought a daughter should be. Every man she had met since had reinforced it. Like she was a magnet for controlling and abusive men, none of whom thought they *were*.

She had seen her mother with small bruises on her arm in the shape of Don's fingers. "He just doesn't know his own strength," Janet had said. And when she had looked at her husband, her face had gone slack with love.

Jennifer had grown up thinking that was how a woman was supposed to act. Forced to save a man from his own ego. Or any other mess he had gotten himself into.

All while pretending not to know it was *her* that did it.

She scanned the churning water, but she couldn't see Mark anywhere. She wasn't being forced to save him. She *wanted* to. It felt like standing on the high dive, but instead of people in the water below shouting at her to just jump already, she bent her knees and pushed off with a smile.

She threw herself into an awkward entry, hitting the water flat on her face with a jarring slap. Using the beacon of the burning SUV to guide her, she was better able to fight the current.

She dove under a burning sheet of metal. Dug her toes into the sand at the bottom and pushed up past it. A revving engine sounded like a secondary fire burning on shore. A headlight flared, bouncing along shore as the Jeep pulled away, spitting sand and gravel behind it.

It sped away, and the taillights looked like glowing eyes receding into the distance. At least they didn't have to worry about Reg and his men anymore. Well, for now.

When her feet could touch bottom, she fell into a floating jog with her hands pulling her along. She turned her back to keep the light of the flames out of her eyes and scanned the water. Random lumps — some burning, some floating. A rainbow slick of fluid rolling along with the waves.

Something thrashed several yards out. A low moan she could barely hear over the crackling fire and sizzling rain.

The memory came to the surface again. "Save me, Tink!"

She sucked in a fresh breath through her teeth and jumped into the current, then swam toward Mark as he floundered against the waves.

She grabbed him around his shoulder — more to steady herself than to hold him up — and he twisted to drive an elbow into her ribs under her right breast. It drove the air out of her lungs and sent a cramp along her side. Her legs felt numb, trailing along behind her.

"It's *me*," she choked.

Her fingers slipped off his shoulders, and she beat at the water with her hands to stay afloat. "Mark!"

Water filled her mouth. She spit it out and took a whooping breath. "Help!"

She felt the wake of his legs kicking to tread water. She didn't want to hit them in case he lost the rhythm and sank. She held her breath and went under.

His hands on her upper arms pulled her up. His fingers dug in, and she thought about the bruises Don left on her mother.

Mark held her in front of him and stared into her face with glassy eyes. He rose out of the water half a foot, and she thought she was flying. When her boots scraped against the concrete again, she almost laughed at herself.

"I'm sorry," he whispered.

As she set her feet on the solid berm under them, she opened her mouth to tell him it was okay, but his stare was focused through her. He looked at something she could never see.

"I'm so sorry," he said.

She put her hands on his face the way he had grabbed her earlier. "Mark."

His gaze settled on hers, but he still wasn't seeing her.

She shook him. "Mark, stop it. *Please*."

He blinked and drew back. When she let her hands fall away, his face crumpled with grief. "Oh, Jesus."

He crushed her against him and wept into her hair. Sobs that shook her with their force, cracking his voice. "I couldn't save them."

"It's okay," she murmured.

"They died, and I couldn't save them."

The sound of him crying into her shoulder was more frightening than running from men trying to kill her. It made her feel lost and helpless.

She continued to tell him it was okay while he cried. It was the only thing she could think to do.

When it seemed like it had finally run its course, she pulled out of his arms. He wouldn't look at her, so she grabbed his chin and pulled his head around to face her.

"It's going to be okay," she said.

"I couldn't save them."

"But you saved *me*."

For a moment, it looked like he was going to break down again, but he took a deep breath and nodded. Without another word, he pulled her back into the water.

He towed her along beside him, a far more powerful swimmer than she had ever been, but when they got to the shallows where he had to walk, he leaned on her as he limped with a hiss of pain with every other step.

The more shallow the water, the more of his weight she supported, until she let him drop to a seat on a smooth rock. He extended his right leg with a moan. Leaned forward with his head down to dig his fingers into the flesh above his knee.

She turned away and staggered toward where the Jeep had been parked. A flickering fire in a bush hissed and sizzled as the rain tried to put it out. She held her hands to it. Stripped the sodden hoodie off to feel the heat on her stomach and back.

As she turned one last time, she saw the dull gleam of a rifle on the ground. Her pistol with a fresh magazine and one still in the pouch, Mark's gun and however much ammo he had left, and now an AR-15. She checked the magazine to find several rounds still in it. Seated it back into the lower receiver and switched the safety on.

When she started back up the shore, she saw Mark on his feet. He grimaced when he put weight on his right leg, but it was keeping him up.

She tied the hoodie around her waist and slung the rifle over her shoulder. Stopped next to him and put her head on his upper arm. "Now what?" she asked.

"Let's fuck 'em up."

She extended her arm into the dark behind them. "Lead the way."

Chapter Twenty-Two

Mark had been lost in his memories. Like when he was caught in another nightmare and he couldn't wake up. He saw the *Northville* all around him. The flat gray walls and pipes. Handrails over the plain grating on the floor.

But he had also seen the glow from the SUV. Heard the sounds of the flames and the gunfire. The Jeep tearing away through the sand.

Then he had heard someone screaming his name. At first, it had been a woman, but it had soon turned into the deep bellow of Captain Jenkins. Screams from below deck and orange flames rolling up the bulkhead.

He waited for the second explosion he knew was coming, but it never did. The one that killed his crew. Friends ... no, *family*. The ones he was supposed to protect.

Caught in the nightmare of his imperfect memory, he had tried to get to the opening that would lead him down to where they were, but no matter how hard he swam, he never made any headway. His name floated up out of the dark, and somebody had grabbed him to try to stop him from going down.

How could they keep him from saving the ones he loved?

When he came back to himself, the confusion had almost made him push away from her, but when he grabbed her, and his feet had found the concrete reef, a cry that had been years in the making bubbled up into his throat.

Even as his shame grew for breaking down in her arms, the sorrow overtook it. He hadn't even cried at the funerals.

When she said that it was okay because he had saved *her*, the grief had subsided. In its place was a raw emptiness ready to be filled by something else. Something more productive.

He had massaged his knee, digging into the scar tissue and getting some heat back into the joint. He straightened his compression socks, a near impossible feat with wet legs. By the time he was standing, Jennifer had come back from warming herself by the fire. When he saw the rifle slung over her shoulder, he had flushed with pride.

He had no right to be proud of someone who was essentially a stranger, but he couldn't stop it. He wanted her to do well, and now that he had saved her life once, he would die to do it again if needed.

For the first time in years, he didn't feel the crushing guilt slowing him down.

He led her into the trees lining the beach. "We'll stay up here and skirt around the entrance from the road," he said.

Her boots clomped along behind him. There was no way for her to be quiet in them, but the rain covered most of the sound.

"Where are we going?" she asked.

"To the marina. It's about a mile out. A short swim at the end."

"How short?"

"A dozen yards or so."

"That's not too bad."

"It *might* be more like twenty-five."

She sighed in disgust. "I'll manage."

"And there are usually crocs around there."

"Great. I should have stayed in the SUV."

"We can go back to the generator shed. I'm sure Brad would help you stay warm."

"He's probably very sweet…" She looked up into the rain. "To his mother."

Mark chuckled under his breath and led her out of the trees to a bulwark of broken concrete stretching out into the water like a crooked peninsula. "We'll walk along this for a bit, and at the head where it spills into the trees, we'll go over and swim for it."

"We can't just walk around?"

"There's a big fence. I'll swim, but I ain't climbing."

"Such a baby."

He walked in a crouch as low as his knee would let him get, and he scanned the marina from over the top of the concrete.

"I thought the power was out," Jennifer said.

"I think it still is." He saw many lights coming from boats in the marina. LEDs and regular security floods. But nothing like the small town of illumination he would expect if the power was back on. "It's all coming from generators. These aren't quiet hours. Besides, with the storm, nobody would really care."

Though he had been caught running his own generator late when he had been tied off to a dock with no shore power. A verbal warning and an order to shut it down, but none of the other boat owners had complained. There weren't many people living there nearly full time like him.

He pointed to a dark patch close to the office. "That's me. I have a spot there for a couple more months, but my buddy is closer to us." He pointed to a big houseboat with light coming from nearly every window. "That's Longjohn. He'll take that thing almost anywhere. Not sure why he's on the boat instead of his RV, but I'm glad. He'll help us."

"Help us with what?" she asked.

"Anything we need."

"But I don't want anybody else involved."

Mark heaved himself up onto the rocks. He reached back for her, but she ignored his hand and ascended on her own. He pulled his hand back to help himself over the pile instead. "St. James Protection. Like private security, right?"

"Yeah."

"Family owned, correct?"

"Right, but I have the majority."

"Unless you're dead, which is the way your husband seems to want you. Is there even a slight chance your parents are involved?"

She tensed like she was about to stomp her foot and shout, but she settled down with a considering nod. "No. Not a chance."

"Then is there a chance they might be in danger, too?"

She looked reluctant to say, but she finally nodded again. "Probably. Yeah, I think so."

"Then you might need help against an enemy with more resources than you."

"Technically, they're *my* resources."

Mark eased down into the water. Even with the rain soaking him from head to foot, it felt so much colder than it had earlier. "Be that as it may, you're gonna need some support. I'm not enough, but I know people."

"Like … what was his name? Longjohn?"

"Yes, he's people, too." He didn't bother asking this time. He just grabbed her waist and lifted her down into the water next to him.

"No," she said. "I can't ask anybody else to get into this. What if he got hurt, or worse?"

She lifted the rifle out of the water as she sunk deeper.

"Look, he was the old harbormaster here. He knows *everybody*. How all the systems work. Who to call and who *not* to talk to. And he makes excellent chili. Besides, I'm fucking pissed, and he will be too."

"But why?"

Mark kicked out to tread water. "Because I don't like what your husband is doing to you. I don't know you, but I feel like you don't deserve it. I *feel* like you're a good person. Plus, like you said, I saved your life, so now I'm responsible for it, right?"

Saying it out loud made him realize that was what he was going to fill the emptiness inside him with. Anger.

"I want to hurt him for hurting you. Also, he blew up my boat, so fuck that guy." He turned to swim away but paddled to turn back to face her again. "Also, you're cute as shit, and I'm a sucker for a pretty face."

He pushed away to swim slowly toward the ladder on the other side of the fence that would lead them up onto the wooden boardwalk. He heard her splash through the water behind him. He looked back, and in the calmer water slowed by the boats and docks, she managed to keep up, even with one hand holding the rifle up.

"Was it the bikini?" she asked.

He thought about how he'd had trouble focusing after seeing her bent over. Like a teenager unable to tear his eyes away from his first Hustler. "I'm not gonna lie. It was distracting."

"That's what Reg wanted. He picked it so you would be distracted."

"*He* picked it?"

"I hate it."

"Then I change my mind. I didn't like it either." He grabbed the bottom rung of the ladder and turned to guide her over. He lifted his good leg to make a ledge for her to stand on. Her smile was a relief. "Besides," he continued. "It made your ass look fat. Use my leg to get going."

She snorted laughter as she grabbed the rung and pulled herself up to put her foot just above his knee. "It was a *string* bikini. How could it make my ass look fat?"

He hissed in a false apology. "I guess it was just your ass, then."

She flipped water into his face before climbing out, but he heard her laughing under her breath the whole way up.

The compulsion to look up at the ass in question was enough to make him clamp his teeth together. He looked to the side as he lifted himself up enough to get his good foot planted on the rung.

He was out of breath by the time he got to the top. If she saw how red his face was, he hoped she thought it was because of the exertion.

Chapter Twenty-Three

Hayes held onto the wheel as he bounced the Jeep over the rough terrain leading back to the access road. He glanced down at the dashboard. Oil pressure low. Heat jumping up.

Steam billowed across the windshield. One headlight sparked off the rain. The other flickered on and off. The sound of it hanging by the wires and knocking against what was left of the brush guard reminded him of a small child knocking on the door to be let in.

At the sound of a gasp in the backseat, Hayes looked into the rearview mirror. Cox rolled his eyes in panic as blood bubbled out of his mouth. He doubled over in a cough, and when he sat back up, more blood poured out to paint his chin red. Crimson trickles from each nostril. Dark circles under his eyes.

"Ah, fuck," Cox whispered.

Hayes shrugged and looked over at Harris. He wasn't much better. Two growing red spots in his chest. Eyes closed. Blue lips. But his nostrils flared with each labored breath.

Hayes looked back out the windshield to drive over the

curb into the lane leading back to the guard shack. "Lucky fucking shots, right?"

Neither of the men answered.

"I told you not to go shooting at the bottom of that thing. Hard to explain that shit, don't you think?"

"Fuck," Cox said.

Hayes shook his head. "Then just running out there without Harris out front covering the windshield. Talking about a *crossfire*? Idiot. And you thought there was no way she could hurt you. Remember what you said?"

Cox had pushed away from the Jeep with a sneer. "No fucking way she can beat me," he'd said. "You can sit back here and sniff her panties all you want, but I'm gonna go take care of business."

Hayes laughed. "And she lit you up. Or at least, *somebody* did. But I've seen her on the courses. Thanks to her Daddy issues, she can get. It. Done."

"Can you shut the fuck up, please?" Harris wheezed.

Hayes looked over with a grin. "Nope. I'm saying my piece. Cuz you two fucked it up, and now I get to sit back — not shot, by the way — and tell you what you did wrong. My favorite part."

Cox moaned. "I need a fucking hospital."

"See," Hayes said, "it was supposed to be easy. Clip 'em both while they were on the boat, then away we go. But Reg had to be an asshole. He always has to be the one. Get the girl. Get the money. Get the credit. And trust me, I understand. He gets 'em wet for some reason. Even the dudes. You see the way the old man drools all over him? You'd think *he* was the one that wanted to marry him instead of his daughter."

Hayes usually didn't mind being on the outside, though. He got to watch, and sometimes play. He would have liked to play with Jennifer a little. She was hot as fuck, and Reg talked about her like she was a plate of green beans.

And the mother? He wasn't much into MILFs, but Janet was enough to change his mind. And the way she took all the abuse the old man gave her? Like Jennifer, it was sexy. "A woman that knows her place is fucking wife material, right?"

Neither one answered.

Maybe when they went up north to sink the old man's stupid yacht, he could have a little fun with her before he threw her overboard.

Then, the company would belong to Reg. They could do anything. As long as Jennifer and her Navy boy didn't fuck things up any worse.

The guard shack appeared out of the rain, and Hayes drove over both lanes to pull into a space for visitors wanting to use the walking path to get to the beach. Nestled the ruined front end into the bushes.

He rolled to a stop and pulled his pistol. Dug the suppressor out of the pouch in his cargo pants. Took his time screwing it on.

"I gotta say, I'm getting a little tired of waiting." He turned to Harris. "I've been promised a lot. Now don't get me wrong. I've gotten my fair share."

He put the barrel under Harris's collar bone, angled down so the bullet would hopefully hit his heart. "I just want more."

He fired twice and spun to put the smoking gun against Cox's stomach. Two shots to make it hurt so he'd double over. Another to the side of the head. The bullet blasted out of his skull and through the seat back. Then a spark from the back when it hit metal.

Hayes shut the Jeep off and got out, dropping the keys in the seat behind him. He reached back inside for the tracking monitor and bent over it to keep it protected from the rain.

He slid the gun into his waistband at the small of his back as he jogged into the shack to meet Lewis, hissing in pain as the hot suppressor touched skin.

He tossed the monitor over as soon as he was out of the rain. "Check it."

Lewis grabbed the case with a nod. He pointed to the small handheld radio on the counter. "Reg is on coms."

Hayes snickered. "So much for radio silence. There been anybody coming through?"

"I had to turn a couple cars away, but it looks like everybody has the good sense to stay home in this shit. I think it should be over soon, though."

Hayes grabbed the radio, but he waited to key it while Lewis did whatever he did to make the monitor work. Hayes had no idea how to use it. That's what they paid other people for.

"So you didn't get her?"

"Not sure. Is her dot floating out to sea?"

"Fuck," Lewis muttered. "No, it looks like she's on the move. South down to what looks like a marina? Yeah, the Sediment Key Marina. Moving slow, but with a purpose."

Hayes snarled as he lifted the radio. "B Team to Home. Come in."

A crackle filled the shack before Reg's voice shouted through the small speaker. "You get the package? Over."

Hayes pulled the distortion away from his face with a grimace. "Negative. Lost two. The package is on the move to the Sediment Key Marina. Over."

"Roger that. Her accomplice is Mark Adler, retired Navy. Recon shows he has a boat moored there. Likely the package's destination. Over."

Hayes rolled his eyes. Why bother with code names

and vague descriptions if he was going to identify their target? "Acknowledged. Will secure new transportation and intercept. Over."

"Roger. Track them and *watch*. Wait for me on site for further instructions. Over."

"What?" Hayes demanded.

"Wait a minute." Reg said. "What do you mean, *new* transportation?"

Hayes lifted the radio like he was going to smash it on the counter. Flashing lights beaming into the shack made him step back to drop down below the counter.

Lewis closed the monitor and stepped out to wave a cop car through with his hat.

Hayes pulled the radio to his lips. "Fuck you. I'm killing this bitch and her Navy boy. They killed Harris and Cox, and it would have been me too if I hadn't been the only fucking competent *man* on the scene."

"Calm down and tell me what happened. Over."

Sirens cut through the storm, and more lights flashed as two more cop cars sped by. Lewis waved them through, still deep in his role as the gate guard.

"Here's what's gonna happen," Hayes barked. "If I can't get another car, I'm gonna walk to the marina. And then I'm gonna kill the Navy boy. And *then* I'm gonna choke your dumb bitch wife to death with my dick. Come get your Jeep at the main gate, and bring a cleaner. Harris and Cox bled all over it before I shot them to put them out of my misery."

He snapped the volume knob down to power the radio off and threw it against the wall. The way it shattered was so satisfying. It calmed him right down. "No way I'm gonna wait and watch. I'm gonna fucking end it."

Lewis covered his ears as a blaring fire truck sped by.

Hayes jumped up to join him as headlights swelled out of the darkness coming from the beach.

Hayes ran over to flag the car down, running up to the driver's window. Inside was an old man and woman dressed in identical beach outfits.

"Hey, have you seen anything like this?" the old man shouted. His grin made his eyes twinkle. "We thought we'd just wait it out, but when something blew up down there, we figured it was time to head out." He pointed behind him with his thumb. "Some of the trees are on fire."

Hayes grabbed his pistol out of his waistband. "That's not good, buddy." He shot the old man in the face. Leaned across and put one in the old woman's temple.

As the car rolled backward, Hayes jerked the door open and dragged the man's body out so he could jump in and hit the brakes. He closed the door and leaned through the window. "Get the fucking tracker and let's go!"

Lewis ducked inside as he shed the high-vis vest. He came out with the monitor cradled against his chest. He handed it to Hayes and jogged around the car. Pulled the old lady out and dropped into her seat.

"There's blood all over."

"So, roll your window down, Let the rain wash it off."

Lewis complied as Hayes hit the gas. They passed another fire truck on their way out.

Chapter Twenty-Four

Jennifer tried not to drop into a tactical crouch as she followed Mark along the boardwalk. He walked with caution, but without intention. Like he was just out stretching his legs. His rolling limp made her wince.

"They patrol out here," he said. "Just keep the rifle on the sling and stay close."

Like he had read her mind.

They passed a long speedboat on their way to Longjohn's houseboat. It was more the type of boat she was used to seeing. Since Don had become rich, he had acted like he thought a rich person was supposed to act. After a while, it was no longer an act.

In addition to expensive speedboats, she was used to seeing much bigger boats. Yachts and cruisers, and one of the things she had always regretted was never learning how to pilot one. Whenever she had asked, Don had said to use the crew. That's what they were paid to do. Deep down, she suspected it was something he thought only men should do.

Now that she thought about it, there were very few female employees at St. James. Receptionists and schedulers. Purchasing agents and assistants. The only ones with any power were her and Janet, and she couldn't fool herself into thinking it was because they were anything more than family. Accessories to his success.

"This is all for service retirees and active members," Mark said. "A lot of them just down here for a few months to escape the northern weather."

The idea of living simply on the water with nothing but the next day to worry about was oddly appealing. No forced workouts or appointments. Just doing whatever she wanted.

She wondered what she would do if she was in that position. She frowned to herself when she couldn't come up with an answer.

"Here we are," Mark said.

He rounded the corner to the walkway leading to the gap in the rope railing where they could board. He dropped down into his knees with a groan of pain. He reached back toward her. "Give me the rifle."

She unslung it and let it hang from the strap. Directed it to his hand so he could grab it. He leaned over the edge of the walkway like he was going to drop it into the water.

"There's a ledge under here for hooks and poles and ropes and shit. I'm putting it here for safekeeping. Going inside armed is okay, but I don't want to freak him out."

When he was finished, he took a deep breath and tensed to get back to his feet, but he dropped back down with a hiss. "Shit. You mind helping me up?"

She jumped forward to grab his arm, throwing it over her shoulder to push against his armpit. He growled through his teeth, but when they were up, he stepped away with a sigh. "Thanks. Sorry."

"Don't be."

"Can't help it."

He swept his arm at the opening in the rail, and she stepped across. The boat gave a little under her weight, but nothing like when she had stepped into Mark's boat. Of course, she could barely feel Don's yacht budge, even when *he* boarded.

Mark eased around her and opened the door. He ducked inside and motioned for her to follow. A few steps into the cabin, and she closed the door behind her while looking around in admiration.

Dark wood paneling and white trim. Brass fixtures, and what looked like slate tile. But what made her catch her breath were the plants. They covered nearly every surface. Vines trailing to the floor. Ferns and cacti. Tomatoes hanging over from the weight of the fruit.

She pointed to one plant in the corner. "Is that weed?"

"Probably." Mark leaned against a nearby counter. "Hey, Johnnie! You home?"

A doorway in the back filled with the shadow of a bear wearing headphones.

"Hey, hey," the bear said. "I'm online with Jordan. GTA 5. We're trying to escape five stars in a food truck."

The bear stepped out into the light to reveal himself to be a huge man covered in hair. A large gray tank top over matching baggie shorts. He reminded Jennifer of Hagrid from the Harry Potter movies. Or maybe Hagrid's father.

"Tell Jordan you got shit to do," Mark said. "Longjohn, we need your help."

Longjohn stared at Mark for a moment before directing his gaze to Jennifer. She was glad the wet hoodie covered her ass, but it left her upper body open to his scrutiny. He didn't look as if he was judging her attractiveness. It somehow felt like he was judging her as a person.

She wished he would just stare at her tits instead.

Longjohn nodded once and turned back to the doorway. She heard him muttering into the microphone dangling from the headphones, but she couldn't pick out any words.

"You're a wizard, Harry," she whispered.

Mark looked back at her in confusion. "What?"

"Nothing."

Longjohn stomped back out to meet them. He pointed at Jennifer. "I don't know you, but I bet you don't always look like that." He turned to Mark. "But I *do* know you, and you look like shit."

In the bright light inside, she took a good look at Mark and had to agree. Where the bullet had grazed his ribs was a furrow of angry raised skin. Knuckles split and bruised. Blood seeping from punctures and slashes in his arm and shoulder. Both elbows scraped raw.

His good knee was scraped open to stain the top of his sock with blood. The right knee looked like a swollen bag of gravel.

She looked at her reflection in the nearest window and gasped in shock. One eyebrow split open, swelling to push her eyelid down. A fresh trail of blood angling down from a gash over her temple. Her hair looked like a soaked rat's nest full of broken straw.

A bruise on her ribs spread up to color her left breast an alarming shade of plum. She looked down at her scraped knees. The cuts and bruises on her hands. A weeping slice down her leg from under the hoodie tied around her waist. It cut through the snake's tail of her tattoo.

Her eyes welled with tears, and her throat closed. She hugged herself and turned away. A hand on her shoulder pulled her back around.

Longjohn stood in front of her, looking down with a kind smile. The sympathy in his eyes only made her cry harder. When he pulled her into his chest, she didn't resist. His hands stroked her back as she bawled all over his shirt.

She hitched in a shaking breath. "He tried to kill me." She sounded like a child trying to explain where the pain was.

"Who did?"

Mark pushed off from the counter. "Her husband. And he tried to kill me too. Blew up my fucking boat."

Longjohn eased her off of his chest, leaving behind a Rorschach blot of tears and blood.

"Don't cry, lady."

"Jennifer," she said.

"Oh, I have a granddaughter named Jennifer. She's also lovely. And that leaves me with a question."

She wiped her eyes and dragged her forearm across her nose with a noisy sniff. "What?"

"Why would anybody want to hurt a pretty thing like you?"

She wanted to bristle at the compliment. She was more than her looks. She was... Jennifer collapsed against him again. It was *her* time to weep uncontrollably.

The man's eyes were true. Full of more love than she — a stranger — deserved, but they were confused. He really didn't understand. He didn't know her, and he thought she was worth something, and it suddenly didn't matter that it was because he thought she was pretty. What *else* did he know about her? Just that, and for him, that was enough.

"Second question."

She stepped back and crossed her arms. "What question is that?"

He cocked his thumb back over his shoulder to point at Mark. "How the hell did you end up with *him*?"

She burst out laughing and dropped her arms. This time, when he hugged her, she hugged him back.

Chapter Twenty-Five

Mark had always thought chili was better after it was heated up. And lasagna. Way better out of the microwave the next day. By the way Jennifer was wolfing it down, she was either starving, or she agreed with him. He had told her Longjohn's chili was good.

He watched her scrape the last bite out of the bowl, sniffing from the spice before scooping it into her mouth. He looked away before he could be caught staring.

Longjohn set a bottle of tequila down, followed by three glasses. A nice reposado with a name Mark couldn't pronounce.

"This first, then some water," Longjohn said.

Mark couldn't agree more, but when he brought the glass to his lips, he hesitated. Jennifer threw hers back and smacked her lips. Longjohn took his usual sip. Mark asked himself if he wanted it or *needed* it.

Even thinking about putting it down gave him the answer. This time, he just wanted it.

He drank it down and sighed the heat out with pleasure. When he pushed his glass away, Longjohn lifted one eyebrow, but he didn't say anything. Instead, he turned to Jennifer. "I've heard of your company."

She leaned back in surprise. "You have?"

"I've even met your father. Don St. James."

"Where? When?"

Longjohn took another sip. "My son is a cop in Louisiana. He was up for training in tactical response inside a crowd, like Mardi Gras or some such. I don't remember the name of the course—"

"Crisis Dispersement," Jennifer offered.

Longjohn nodded before continuing. "A fairly idiotic name, but fine. It was a weeklong course only a few years ago."

"Yeah, I wasn't there. I was running a kill house in Dallas."

Mark didn't know what a kill house was, but Longjohn seemed to understand.

"Jonathan said the training was fine, but there were a few instructors he didn't care for. One had a black pompadour. He said he bragged constantly, running his mouth more about himself instead of about the course."

Jennifer's face burned as she looked down. "That was Reg. Before he was my husband."

"Meaning it happened before he was your husband? Or his behavior has changed since becoming your husband."

She sighed. "No, he's still an asshole. I don't know why I ever…"

When she trailed away, Longjohn waited patiently, but Mark couldn't do it. He felt like he had to fill the silence for her. "Hey, the last time Jonathan was here, did he leave any clothes?"

Longjohn looked over at him like he had farted. "I

believe so. Shorts and t-shirts. Summer stuff. Help yourself."

Mark stood up. "I'm gonna clean up, then."

Longjohn joined him. "I'll get the first-aid kit."

"My parents made me call them by their first names," Jennifer said. "But I think it was mostly my dad who wanted it that way."

Longjohn finished his tequila before gently setting the empty glass down. "If you'll pardon me saying, he seemed a domineering man when I met him. Very full of himself."

She nodded. "But you probably never met my mother, Janet. I remember that she had to stay in the room until the bruises on her face went down enough to cover with makeup. When I got back, she told me that he hit her for *flirting* with the cops that came for training. Something he was always sensitive about, even though he expected us both to do it because it was good for business. She said not to blame him, though. She should have acted right. Exactly how she said it. 'I should have acted right.'"

Longjohn rested his hand on her shoulder. She tilted her head like she was going to rest her cheek on his knuckles but stopped short of contact.

"That's what I saw in Reg," she said. "He was like my father, and I needed to act right for him."

"For him. Your father or for Reg?"

"Does it matter?"

Mark felt like he had walked in on strangers having sex. He wanted nothing more than to backpedal and forget what he saw. "I'll be back."

His knee kept him from running.

"Can I have more chili?" Jennifer asked.

"Of course."

Longjohn said more, but it was lost after Mark shut the door to the bedroom. He opened the closet and dug through the clothes Jonathan had left until he found a suitable outfit. Long black cargo shorts and a black long-sleeved swim shirt. Even a pair of clean boxer briefs.

As he cleaned up in the bathroom, he wondered why hearing Jennifer talk about the abusive men in her life bothered him so much. Was it because he was attracted to her? Because he thought she was a good person, and good people didn't deserve to be treated like that?

Or was it because he *liked* her? The secondhand embarrassment felt for a friend. Or a lover.

He rolled his eyes at himself in the mirror. "Jumping the gun, Mark."

He knew what it was like to say something to somebody that you didn't want to admit. The *real* reason he quit going to therapy.

He put the underwear and shorts on, but he left the shirt until after he'd put something on all of his cuts and scrapes.

Their murmured voices drew him out, and when he rejoined them at the table, he reached to take her hand. "I'm so sorry that all of this is happening to you. Or anything that happened to you before. I'm serious."

She looked at him with a puzzled frown, but she didn't take her hand away. "Thank you."

He sat up straight and turned to face Longjohn. His friend looked back with an approving smile. "Okay, okay," Mark said. "Let's finish up here so we can open your footlocker."

Longjohn laughed, but Jennifer looked confused. "What's in the footlocker?"

Longjohn slid out of his chair to drop to a knee next to Mark. He slid the first-aid kit over and lifted Mark's arm to get a better view of the wound along his ribs.

"Various implements of war," he said. "I always say, a

man prepared is a man survived. Not syntactically accurate, but the message is clear."

Mark bit back a grunt when the cold alcohol pads hit his skin.

Jennifer sat back with a considering look on her face. "And that's what we're doing? Going to war?"

"You're goddamned right," Mark said.

"But why do something like that for me?"

Mark thought about how he had cried in her arms. He sighed in resignation. He repeated what Reg had told him with a sarcastic sneer. "We're all friends here, right?"

Jennifer waited as if he had said nothing. Longjohn finished taping the gauze down. He stood up to walk to Mark's other side to tend to the upper arm and shoulder.

"It's like this," Mark said. "I'm just gonna tell the truth."

"Then get on with it," Longjohn said.

Mark continued without acknowledging the interruption. "For a long time, I thought I wasn't worth being around. I always believed I should have died on the *Northville* along with the ones … who didn't make it. And maybe I still do. But that's not the point. I met you, and I didn't like you." He held his hand up like he anticipated her to defend herself, but she remained silent. Her steady gaze was unnerving.

"I thought you were showing off for *you*. Or for your husband, but not in the way — like he *made* you do it, but…"

He covered his face with his free hand. "I was wrong about you. Like I think you're wrong about yourself. You may not agree, but you saved *me* first. And you let me know it was okay, because I had saved you. The thing I had been trying to do since beating myself up for not being able to save the others. For the first time, the noise of my self-sabotage was barely a whisper in the back of my mind. I could hear myself think again, and the thought that you don't think you deserve it any more than I did makes me so fucking mad. So yes, we're going to war. Because, whether you want it or not, or if you accept it or not, I'm going to protect you. I'm going to keep you safe. Not because you're pretty or have a fantastic body or … any *other* superficial detail you want me to list — and let me tell you, there's a list — but because you taught me that something was more important to me than I thought."

"What?" she whispered.

Mark uncovered his eyes to see her looking at him with curiosity. He had expected tears. Wide-eyed hope. Anything other than clinical expectation.

He forced himself to say it. "My life."

Then he stood without checking to see if Longjohn was finished, pulled the shirt over his head, and walked back to Longjohn's office.

Chapter Twenty-Six

Jennifer watched Mark stalk away. She had never had another person, especially a man, speak to her with such raw emotion before. How could she possibly respond to that?

Longjohn pointed to the first-aid kit. "I can treat any of the places you can't reach. I swear I won't look."

"That wouldn't be very effective, would it?" She stood up and untied the sleeves of the hoodie. Wadded it up on the chair and turned to aim the long slash on her hip at him.

When she bent over to brace on the table, he said, "Dear Lord."

She looked back over her shoulder to see him looking at her butt. She forgot there was nothing there but a string. Even as her face began to burn, she burst out laughing.

The alcohol he slapped on the cut stopped the laughter cold.

Every time he made contact, he apologized and blew on it like she was a child with a scrape on her shin. When he got down to the back of her knee, her stomach hurt from holding in more laughter.

"It looks worse than it is," he said.

"My ass?"

"What? No! That's just fine. I mean—"

She screamed laughter. She turned around and put her hands on his shoulders. His embarrassed shock had turned to a relieved chuckle. "Does it need a bandage or anything?"

He let her help him up. "No, I think it will be fine now that it's clean."

"Then I think I can handle the rest myself."

"Very good." He closed the first-aid kit and slid it into her hands. "My daughter-in-law also has some clothes. I think they should fit, although they might be a little tight." He waved his hands over his chest.

Her face heated up as she laughed again. She figured she sounded like a crazy person, but she couldn't stop.

He joined in, and they both shared a moment that evaporated all the tension and embarrassment. Just two people making the best of a bad time.

"Can you show me?" she asked.

"Of course."

He led her to the room Mark had changed in. To a closet full of clothes. He pointed to the left side. "That's hers."

When he turned to leave her, she grabbed his shirt to stop him. "Can you stay? Like, right outside the door? Just to be close. Please?"

"Absolutely. I'll be right outside."

She watched him leave, but rushed over as he closed the door. "Not all the way! Leave it open a little."

He stopped the door a couple inches from the jamb. "How's that?"

"Sorry, I'm just not ready to be alone yet. "

"I understand."

She went back to the closet and pulled out a pair of khaki shorts. A little longer than Reg would have liked, but they would do. They burned going over the scrapes, but the waist was a perfect fit. The legs were a little tight over the muscle she had built, but they wouldn't restrict her.

A black t-shirt that was way too small across the chest like Longjohn had said, but at least she was covered. And shoes! A pair of pink Crocs that were exactly her size. She put the strap into SPORT mode and slid into them with a sigh. So comfy.

"Can you come in now?"

Longjohn stepped in and looked at her with an apologetic smile. "Well, it is what it is."

She smiled. "It's great."

She stepped into the bathroom and ran the water to get it warm. The boat's pump hummed under the floor. Longjohn sat on the small bed. She grabbed the comb off the vanity. She wondered if Mark had used it. While she combed her hair out, she glanced into the bedroom.

"How did Mark hurt his leg? It had something to do with, what was it, the *Northville*?"

"It did."

She leaned into the mirror to tend to the cut in her temple.

"It was a cruiser he was stationed on. One of the crewmembers had significant undiagnosed mental issues and wanted to hit his personal power button by sabotaging the ammunition stores. The explosion killed several men, including the commander of the boat. It injured several others, and Mark was one of them."

It sounded like he was reciting a report.

"It was one of *his* crewmen, in fact. He blamed himself

for not seeing it in time, thinking he could have somehow prevented it, but he won't admit he was wrong. He still blames himself, and probably always will."

She was sorry she'd asked. While holding pressure against the gash on her head, she leaned out to tell him to stop, but he continued before she could say anything.

"A piece of metal handrail flew up from below decks and shattered his knee. The fire burned both of his feet, melting the soles of his shoes right off. But the worst was the compartmental syndrome the blow caused in his calf. So much swelling they had to open it up or lose the leg altogether. I sometimes wonder if he wouldn't have been better off. Anyway, they removed a significant portion of muscle in his calf, rebuilt the knee, and sent him home."

She went back to the mirror and moved to the split in her eyebrow. It just needed a tiny waterproof bandage, but when she was done, her head pounded with every beat of her heart. It felt like she was about to vomit.

"Thank you for staying with me. And thank you for telling me about him."

"Oh, I barely scratched the surface. Most of it is his story to tell. I just gave you the back-of-the-book version."

She nodded and leaned against the sink as a wave of vertigo swept through her. "I understand. Umm … can I be alone now? I'm sorry, but—"

"No need to apologize. I understand."

He left, and she closed the bathroom door.

How was somebody supposed to recover from that? *She* certainly didn't have the answer. She didn't know if she would ever be able to live out from under the shadows of her parents. Away from Reg's memory. All the men she had let hurt her.

She looked at her reflection. The cuts and bruises she

deserved, but the long hair she despised. Just because Reg liked it that way.

She pulled it into a tail and jerked it back like she could pull it off her head, but the stab of pain brought up fresh nausea. She reached for the vanity drawer with a growl. If there were scissors in there, she would cut it off. Just hack it away until she could see herself again.

But she let her hand fall to her side as the tail slipped through her fingers.

She didn't even know who she was. Would she recognize herself if the real Jennifer showed up?

And the bikini she wore under her borrowed clothes. Stupid strings, and fabric that barely covered her nipples. Or the makeup everybody demanded that she wore. Or the dumb fucking seashell earrings.

She reached up and snatched them out of her ears. Put them both in the palm of her right hand and shook them like dice.

She hated them. Hated Reg for making her wear them. Hated herself for letting him dictate her life. She drew her arm back and threw them as hard as she could into the sink.

She closed her eyes against the bits of shattered shell that flew back into her face. Bent over the sink and cried. Maybe it would have been better if Reg had killed her on the boat.

She remembered Mark telling her he had remembered how important his life actually was because she had saved him. How could he possibly think anything good about her?

She wiped her eyes and looked back at her reflection. "That's bullshit, and you know it."

She forced herself to smile.

"You are a good person, but not for him. Not for *anybody*. For *you*."

The smile almost felt real. She looked down into the sink. Bits of shell and gold … and something else. Bile rose into her throat as she picked up a tiny circuit. One of a lot of trackers she herself had purchased three months ago. A model Reg had insisted on.

He knew where she was.

He had known all along.

Chapter Twenty-Seven

Mark carried an armload of weapons and ammo to the table. He passed Longjohn standing outside the other bedroom door. He wanted to stop and ask what the hell was going on, but his friend gave him a small shake of his head.

Mark pushed the bottle of tequila out of the way. Set the guns down and turned for a drink of water instead. Longjohn's filter made it taste like it was charged with electricity. Almost cold enough to form ice on the surface, it made his teeth ache. He stopped to catch his breath, closing his eyes against the dull throbbing in the center of his forehead. The next drink he took a little slower.

He inspected his haul from Longjohn's footlocker. The man liked his 1911s. Two .45s with four magazines each. Black molded holsters with a waistband clip. He added the 9mm pistols they got from Reg's men. Four magazines, two of which needed reloading.

The KA-BAR and one stainless steel multi-tool, because why not?

As he slotted fresh rounds into the empty magazines, he heard Jennifer ask Longjohn if he would come into the bedroom with her. He leaned back to get a better angle on the door so he could listen.

He soon wished he hadn't bothered.

Longjohn told an antiseptic version of his story. One that left out the clues Mark had missed leading up to the explosion. The dark depths of his psyche afterward. The way he had wished more than anything to die so he wouldn't have to live with the guilt.

The months of agonizing surgeries and physical therapy.

Hearing somebody else tell his personal story felt like a betrayal, but Longjohn had been there for him during the worst of it. If anybody deserved to relay his pain to another, it was Longjohn.

He couldn't remember a truer friend, or somebody he loved more. With the last bullet slotted into the magazine, Mark promised himself to not let another day go by without telling him how much he meant to him.

Longjohn stepped out of the bedroom and eased the door shut behind him with a sad smile and stooped shoulders. He walked in and grabbed the tequila. Poured two glasses without asking Mark if he wanted it.

Instead of sipping it, Longjohn slammed it back and reached for the bottle again.

Mark knocked half of his back and swiped his hand over the glass when Longjohn moved to pour more into it. "I'm good."

Longjohn sat down and shot the second glass. He sighed and leaned back. "Well, *she's* not."

"What do you mean?"

"That little girl's hurting."

"Little girl?"

Longjohn waved him away. "Please. At my age, all of you are babies."

Mark finished his tequila and put the glass in the sink to close the temptation. "Is she okay?"

"I don't think so. She needs to be saved, but she doesn't want a savior."

"I know how that feels."

Longjohn leaned forward, his brow wrinkling in confusion. "Why would somebody want to hurt her? I just don't understand."

"You also don't really know her."

Longjohn looked at him like he was spouting gibberish. "Really? You telling me you can honestly see her as anything other than how she's acted right here? That she's somehow bad enough that someone wants to kill her?"

Mark dropped into the opposite seat. "I asked myself the same thing. She seems so competent and capable, but still…"

"Childlike," Longjohn said. "Like she hasn't seen enough evil in the world to be able to identify it. But that's not true, because I can see it in her eyes that she knows."

"I think she just got mixed up with the wrong guy. One like her father, from what it sounds like."

"And he wants to own St. James Protection?"

Mark shrugged. "I guess, but it would seem like he has the perfect slice of pie already, if you'll excuse the expression. Part of the company — part of the *family* — and he has *her* to come home to?"

Longjohn steepled his fingers together. His eyes lost focus as he stared into space. "So, he kills her, making it look like an accident. *No…* making it look like a murder. Then he gets her shares of the company. And he has a further plan to do the same to her parents?"

Mark scrubbed his hands over his face. "I guess?"

Longjohn held up a finger. "I will bet my retirement that her husband has taken out a policy on them all. Being in the private security business is dangerous. What would life insurance pay if they died violently instead of peacefully in their sleep?"

Mark dropped his hands from his face. "That actually makes sense. It's psychotic, but it makes sense. He kills them and gets the company, but the policies pay out who knows how much money. Is that all it is? Some long scam?"

Longjohn pointed to the closed bedroom door. "Look at what he enjoyed while he waited for his plan to come together."

"But we've already fucked his plan up. There's no way he can convince anybody to believe his story now."

"I don't think it matters. He has to kill you both now. He can't afford to let you tell anybody the truth. He may still be able to salvage this, and besides, there are still the parents."

Mark stood up. "Then we have to kill him first."

"Or run."

"What? Why would I run?"

"Because it gets her out of harm's way. Take your boat up the coast. I'll follow. We can call right now through my network—"

"Wait a minute," Mark said. "Cell tower's down. How the hell are you on the internet?"

"I have Starlink. How do you think I was online playing video games?"

"Shit, I didn't even think about it. Okay, when she gets out, we'll try to get a hold of her parents. Then we'll pull the anchor and hit the water. Meet them somewhere. Figure it all out."

"Perfect. But right now, we can contact the authorities.

You should have done that the second you came on board."

Mark had lived with a woman that had constantly lectured him about how he *should* have done something. Ever since, whenever somebody did the same — well-meaning or not — he thought of her.

Paula Davis had gone to the same rehab, only two floors up. The concussion from an IED blast had blown out one of her eardrums. An eye filled with blood for four weeks, and lasting brain trauma. Once the physical damage had healed, there was nothing to tell anybody she had a major disability.

Balance issues and nerve pain. Depression and anger. But she was painfully funny, and her laugh had sent shivers down his spine. A beast in the gym with a body to match — lean and firm — and short hair she kept dyed a copper red.

He fell for her the second he saw her when he limped into the elevator on its way carrying her down to the lobby.

They had both needed something to lean on, so they picked each other, and at first the support was perfect. So what if the pain and PTSD made them snap at each other every once in a while. Or if the nightmares kept each other awake. The conversations were amazing, the sex was fantastic, and they both wanted nothing more than to get through the bullshit of their pasts to get on with the future. Only neither knew what that future was supposed to be.

It wasn't long before they both realized their respective futures didn't have the other one in them. He criticized her for covering everything with humor, even as he continued to laugh at her jokes. Mostly inappropriate, but always hilarious. Nothing was off-limits, and it got her in trouble.

She told him what he should have done after every mistake, even though it was too late to change it.

"You should have been in the other lane."

"Why didn't you take the other bag with you so you wouldn't have to take two trips?"

"If you liked it so much, why didn't you buy two of them?"

"You should have asked for a military discount."

The weight of the constant second-guessing had become a burden, but nothing too heavy to carry, until she started in on the *Northville*.

"You should have told your commander."

"Why didn't you pull that sailor aside?"

"Should you have done something sooner?"

"You shouldn't keep your head down and just keep going."

They echoed his criticism of his own behavior so closely — things he wasn't ready to answer for himself — that they started to sting. The stinging got worse, and he felt attacked. Finally, he retaliated, and the argument brought up every fear and regret they each had, and when they were done, they knew the door could never be closed again.

They had crossed a line they couldn't go back over.

The relationship ended quietly. He moved out, and he never saw her again. If he had been willing to answer his own questions, he might have been able to answer hers. Maybe they would still be together.

It had taken years before he could hear that *coulda shoulda* bullshit without bristling. But he still thought of her. Paula Davis speaking through Longjohn's mouth. "Well, we didn't know you had internet access, because we were busy bleeding and stuff," Mark growled. Maybe he still bristled a *little* bit.

Longjohn held his hands up. "Not a criticism. Just a fact. I didn't think of it, either."

The bedroom door banged open, and Jennifer jumped through. The look of horror on her face made Mark reach for one of the guns, but she held something out in front of her. Like she was offering her baby up for a kiss.

"I'm sorry," she said in a harsh whisper. "I didn't know, I'm sorry."

Mark peeked over her fingertips to see a small circuit in the middle of what looked like shell fragments. He looked up at her empty earlobes. He knew what it meant immediately.

"That's how they found us so easy," he said.

Jennifer let the tracker fall from her hands. "Please, I didn't know."

Mark cursed himself for not thinking of it sooner. She had been wearing so little, he couldn't have imagined where a tracker could have been hidden on her.

The lights dimmed as the generator chugged to a stop.

The rain hitting the windows sounded like a tidal wave.

"Should have had that second drink," Longjohn said.

Jennifer dropped into a crouch as soon as the lights went dark. Mark was proud of her for not screaming. He lowered down to join her, but his knee gave out, and he slammed into the table.

"Motherfucker," he hissed.

Jennifer lunged forward and grabbed one of the pistols. Released the magazine and held it up to the meager light coming through the windows to see if it was loaded. Rammed it back and racked the slide.

Longjohn dropped over his arms like a kid sleeping at his desk. He reached for a gun but snatched his hand back when glass shattered, and a bullet struck the table.

The cough of another suppressed shot, and Longjohn threw himself back with a cry of pain. Blood arced up from his head, and his chair tipped over to dump him out on the floor.

Mark jumped over and spread out to cover his body, but Longjohn pushed him off with a growl. He sat up with blood streaming down his face. His teeth burned in the center of a crimson mask. He was pissed.

Good.

Chapter Twenty-Eight

Another suppressed shot, and the tequila bottle exploded. Guns and ammos scattered off the table to the floor. Mark crouched down farther and crawled to meet Jennifer under the table.

"Go out the back," Longjohn said, then to Jennifer: "Give me your gun. I'll cover you."

"What? No. Mark tried that shit earlier."

Longjohn ignored her protest. He grabbed Mark's sleeve. "Exit through the kitchen to the stern. Get to your own boat and stick with the plan."

"What plan?" Jennifer asked.

Longjohn held his hand out to her, and she shook her head, even as she dropped her pistol into his palm. "This is bullshit."

More shots broke more windows. Shattered glass tinkled down in a glittering cascade.

"It's obvious he wants us distracted while somebody approaches from a different direction," Longjohn said. He crawled through broken glass toward the broken windows.

He looked back over his shoulder at Jennifer. "Keep my friend alive, okay? He's a good one."

He winked at Mark before crawling to a position that covered the side door.

Mark grabbed Jennifer and pulled her toward the back. His bad leg dragged near uselessly behind him, but he was able to get his weight on it and stand up in a crouch next to the back door.

He pushed her behind him and cracked the door open. A man holding a suppressed pistol climbed over the stern railing.

Mark didn't wait for him to put his foot on board. He threw the door open and charged across the deck to throw himself into a tackle in the center of the man's chest that carried them both off the boat.

They sailed through the air to land against the edge of the dock, the man's back hitting with a wet crack, cushioned by Mark's forearm.

Mark's hand went numb as they slid into the water.

The man lost his pistol, but still had some fight in him. He thrashed against Mark, catching him in the face and neck with a few decelerated blows as they surfaced.

The man pushed away with a cry of pain. Dipped his hand underwater to bring it back out holding a small knife. The back of Mark's head whacked off the hull of Longjohn's boat as the man surged forward to drive the knife into the meat of Mark's left trapezius muscle.

Bitter cold ran down his arm, and his neck spasmed, banging his temple against the handle of the knife.

The man let go, struggling to stay above water. His face twisted with pain. Mark reached across his body for the knife but couldn't quite reach it and stay floating at the same time. He pushed off the boat and reached for the man, who was paddling toward the ladder on the sidewall.

Mark slapped his hand on the side of the man's head and dug his thumb into his eye. The man screamed and grabbed Mark around the throat.

Mark hitched in a quick breath before the pressure cut it off. He pushed harder with his thumb and wrapped his legs around the man's waist. They dropped under the water, and the man let go as he flailed his arms in a panic to get back to the surface.

Mark pulled his thumb out and hugged the man to his stomach. Looped his hand around the back of the man's neck until his fingers brushed the handle of the knife.

His lungs burned, and his throat ached. Surrounded by darkness, he had no idea how close they were to the bottom.

With a final push, he got his fingers around the knife. He pulled it out, and the slicing pain made him blow his air out in a growl through his nose. He brought the knife around into the space between them, and the man doubled his efforts to swim away.

Mark released the hold he had with his legs, and as he drifted away, he drove the knife up through the water. His strike was blind, but he felt it hit. The knife stabbed into the flesh under the man's jaw. It lodged in his upper palate, and Mark heard the last of the man's breath leave in a bubbling scream of pain.

Mark kicked him in the chest and took a moment to orient himself. Faint light above. Just a flicker to guide him, and he kicked toward the surface.

Water streamed past his ears in a rush that sounded like wind in a microphone. He couldn't see the lights anymore. Couldn't tell if he was still going up. His throat fought against him to pull in air.

He tucked his chin to his chest to keep his last bit of air inside and reached for another pull against the water when his knuckles cracked against the bottom of Longjohn's boat.

The top of his head was next. The impact sounded like somebody dropped a brick onto cracked asphalt. The dark water became a seamless void of white light.

He floundered against the hull, spinning and turning to find his way to the air his mind screamed for.

He heard the screams and smelled the smoke. Dropped his arms and prepared to sink down into the flooded compartments below him to die with the rest of his crew.

Something pushed against his side. Hands crawled over his chest. He tried to knock them away, but his arms wouldn't follow his commands. Were they somebody else's?

Arms wrapped around him. Pressure against his back. Rising toward the surface felt like flying.

He hit the air, and his jaw unlocked. He opened his mouth as wide as it would go, and he took in air so sweet, it hurt his teeth, only to double over and cough into the water.

"Grab the ladder," Jennifer said.

He reached, but his hand missed. He tried again, and his fingertips skimmed off the aluminum. He dipped under the surface. Jennifer went under with him to push him back up. She gasped in a fresh breath. "Grab the fucking ladder!"

His left hand didn't seem to be working, so he let go of Jennifer to throw out the right one. The bottom rung slapped into his hand, and he pulled himself to the wall with Jennifer hanging off his neck. She panted in his ear as he tried to lift himself up, but he collapsed back with a moan.

"Hang on," she said. Her feet dug into his hips, and she climbed up his body to get to the rungs over his head.

Her final step was on his shoulders, and she hoisted herself to the top.

When she bent down and extended her hand to him, he shrugged his left shoulder up to get his hand to come out of the water. Gritting his teeth with the effort, he got his fingers up to hers. Her grip ground the bones in his hand together as she braced herself and pulled.

His shoulder creaked in protest, but her effort was enough to get him out of the water so he could use his legs.

When he joined her on the boardwalk, he saw they were two boats up from Longjohn's spot. She spun to run back, but Mark stopped her.

"No," he said. "He's doing what he's doing so we can get away."

She stared for a moment, and her eyes widened in understanding.

The thinning clouds let the sun through to brighten the docks. It looked like the artificial light of a night game.

She nodded and grabbed his hand. Mark pulled her away and headed for his houseboat.

He wondered if Longjohn was okay. He could tell Jennifer was crying, and he was glad the rain was still heavy enough to hide his own tears.

Chapter Twenty-Nine

Mark guided her along the dock, or rather, she held him up while he steered. She hated being out in the open, and she looked back to see what was happening behind her. Longjohn's windows were still dark.

"That's the Harbormaster's office," Mark said.

Jennifer faced front and saw a dark lump of stucco forming out of the shadows.

"Turn right just after it. That's where my boat is."

She pushed him away from the edge of the board-walk. His limp seemed to be getting worse. She looked over at him, and his eyelids drooped like he was fighting sleep.

Beams of light danced out from behind the office. Flashlights coming around to shine into her face.

Jennifer slid to a stop and looked away. Mark leaned against her with a muttered curse. He tensed like he was going to bolt, but she held him back.

It couldn't have been Reg's men. They wouldn't give up their positions like that. It had to be residents. Maybe a patrol of some kind.

She rose on her tiptoes and whispered into Mark's ear. "Act drunk."

"No problem."

The light dipped from her face to form a pool at her feet. Two young sailors dressed in camouflage uniforms spread apart. One put his hand on his holstered firearm. The other held up one hand and waved. Before he could say anything, the rain stopped.

At first, she could still hear it hitting the water out past the boats, but soon there was nothing but the wind. She put her hand out with her palm up, but when there were no drops splashing into it, she smiled. It was finally over.

"Hot damn," Mark said.

The sailor with his hand up shook his head like he was clearing his thoughts. "How you folks doing tonight — today?"

He seemed friendlier than she expected. But why wouldn't he be? The marina was for service members and whoever they brought with them.

Then she glanced at the other sailor with his hand on his gun. Of course, Reg and his men could get in here, too. Plus, there had been an explosion just a couple miles away. She told herself to make it a good one. She wished she hadn't put on the clothes from Longjohn. She could use a little distraction on her side.

"Not great," Jennifer said. "My boyfriend's drunk. He fell in, and I had to drag him out."

The other sailor dropped his hand off his holster. He shook his head with a smile. "You pulled him out on your own?"

"Well, he helped a little."

The first sailor walked over and ducked down to look up in Mark's face. His eyes widened in surprise. "Adler?"

Mark continued to act drunk, and he looked at the

soldier with an exaggerated squint. "Drake? Holy shit, I didn't recognize you without a lobster in your hand." He turned to Jennifer. "We went out over a long weekend with nothing but our kayaks and wetsuits, and all we did was catch and eat lobster."

Drake straightened up with a grin. "And drank beer." He looked at Jennifer. "I can see why you might be having a little trouble with him. I've had to pick him up enough to know what it's like."

Drake turned back to shout over his shoulder, "This is that dude that'll show you more fish in a day than you've seen all your life."

"Uh huh." The other sailor didn't seem impressed.

Jennifer wanted to scream in frustration. Reg was probably on his way right now. The thought of asking the two sailors for their help flashed into her mind, but it felt wrong to put anybody else in danger, even if they *could* protect her … or throw her in jail.

"Hey," Jennifer said. She pulled Mark closer. "I don't want to be rude, but we were on our way to something."

Drake looked at her with polite curiosity. "What's that?" He apparently couldn't take a hint.

"To *bed*. I was taking him to bed."

The other sailor laughed into his hand. "Dumbass."

Drake nodded in sudden understanding and shuffled back to give them room. He swept his arm along the boardwalk. "Be my guest."

Mark pointed down the pier like Forrest Gump. "That's my boat."

Jennifer waved as she pulled Mark into motion.

"We heard a ruckus out here," Drake said. "Was that you?"

"Maybe. He made some noise going over. I screamed

and jumped in after him. Sorry. But if you hang around, we're about to make some more."

The other sailor laughed. "That's okay. Enjoy yourselves. Just try to keep it down."

Jennifer sagged with relief when they turned around to go back behind the office.

"Taking me to bed, huh?" Mark said.

"Jesus, I thought they were gonna shoot us."

"Nah, somebody probably heard the noise of falling in or the breaking glass. Or me hitting my head on the bottom of the boat."

She hissed in sympathy. "Is it bad?"

"Not as bad as my shoulder. That fucker stabbed me."

"What?" She stopped in shock, and her feet tangled with his. He kept her from going down, but they swung off course, and she had to hang on or else go over into the water.

Mark steadied her. "It was just a little bitty knife. Hurt like hell, though."

"Let's get you inside and take a look."

"Not sure if we have time if we're going to bed first."

"We're *not* going to bed."

She pulled him into motion and led him to the opening in the railing next to his boat. She hopped over and turned around to reach back to help him over.

He shook his head in disappointment. "That's too bad."

"What is?"

"Not going to bed with you."

She looked at his spreading smile.

"Could have used a nap," he said.

She grabbed his wrist and pulled him over to join her. "If that had *really* been my plan, there wouldn't have been much sleeping, I guarantee it."

He limped toward his door and looked back at her with a scandalized smile. "Whatever does that mean?"

She rolled her eyes as she pushed him. She couldn't believe they were both acting like this while getting ready to fight for their lives. "Can we get on with it, please?"

"I thought you said we *weren't* going to bed."

"That's not what I mean."

She followed him into an interior that almost matched Longjohn's. More dated and fewer plants, but close enough she could navigate it by the memory of the other. "Take your shirt off."

"Reconsidering, are you?"

"I want to see where he stabbed you."

Mark shook his head and lifted his arms over his head in a stretch. His smile faded into anger as he brought his hands back down. "It's fine for now. Let me start the engine so we can unhook."

He was more stable when he turned to walk down the central hallway that led past the bedrooms and to the front of the boat. After a few moments, she felt a rumble shake the floor. Glass clinked in the cabinets behind her.

Mark rushed back through in a crooked jog. "Normally, I secure everything before moving, but I think we'll make an exception." He motioned for her to follow him outside. "Come on. I'll need your help."

As she followed, she wondered what had happened to Longjohn. Whatever it had been, it couldn't have been bad, or they would have gotten a bullet in the back on their way down the boardwalk.

She told herself it was going to be okay, but no matter how hard she tried, she just couldn't believe herself.

Chapter Thirty

When Lewis had moved along the pier to jump into the back of the houseboat, Hayes had hidden between a fueling station and a trash can to cover the windows with his pistol. He could see the Navy boy inside talking to a fat old mountain. Drinking tequila and having just a grand time.

As soon as Jennifer ran up to them with something in her hands, Lewis cut the generator. Hayes would have liked another second to try to figure out what she had been trying to show them, but it was more fun to start shooting.

Out of the three figures, only one of them had a big enough silhouette to see. The old guy's shaggy head sticking up above the table.

Hayes' first shot had been perfect. He was sure he had hit his target, but the old guy had popped up like it had been nothing. Hayes laid down fire to distract them with breaking glass to give Lewis time to get inside, but the Navy boy was already moving.

Hayes saw Lewis and the Navy boy fly overboard to

splash into the water, followed by Jennifer jumping the gap and climbing down the ladder. He had to make sure the old guy was down for the count before going in after them.

As he jumped to the houseboat's deck, the giant inside stood up with a gun, sweeping the windows for intruders. Hayes fired the last two bullets in his magazine, and when one of them hit the old guy in the arm, he almost threw his head back to cackle with excitement.

The shot made the old guy drop his weapon and stumble back. More than enough opportunity to get inside and get it done.

Hayes threw his pistol behind him and crashed through the broken door. His momentum carried him into the kitchen, straight into the old guy's chest.

It was like hitting a tree, but he still drove him back into a plant covered shelf. Dirt and pottery exploded on impact.

Hayes drew back and drove his fist up into the old guy's gut, but all he got was a soft grunt before the old guy hit him with a chopping overhead blow that caught him at the base of his neck.

Hayes dropped to one knee as his arm went numb. A shock of pain cramped under his jaw, sending white spots to dance in front of his eyes.

The old guy rocked back to get space between them. Hayes got his feet under him and sprang up to crack the old guy's jaw with the top of his head.

Hayes staggered back in a daze, but the old guy tumbled over to hit the deck with a jarring *thud*. Hayes shook his head to clear it, snarling in pain when the cramp in his neck twisted through the muscle again.

The old guy scraped his hands through broken glass to push off the floor, but his wobbly arms let him down, and he landed back on his face. Hayes jumped forward and grabbed a double handful of the old guy's shirt.

Flipped him over like he was rolling a whale back into the surf.

Hayes dropped on the old guy's stomach in an aggressive mount and brought both hands down in hammer blows to the old guy's forehead and nose.

A crunch of bone, and blood splashed up into Hayes's eyes as he lifted his hands for another strike.

"You modderfugger," the old man growled.

Hayes curled into the next blow, but both of his arms stopped against the iron crossbar of the old guy's forearm lifted in a block. It felt like he had tried to hit the bumper of an old truck.

The old guy stretched his other hand out into the dark, and Hayes suddenly didn't feel like laughing anymore.

LONGJOHN BLINKED blood out of his eyes. His initial shock and confusion evaporated into anger. When he hit the floor, he floundered like he was in the water. He was aware of the pain in his hands from scraping through broken glass, but the pain felt like it was coming from far away.

Then the feeling of getting turned over. The breath crushed out of him as the asshole dropped onto his stomach. Then the bright shatter of pain when his nose broke, filling the back of his throat with burning copper.

He saw the shape of his attacker lifting his arms for another blow, and Longjohn's senses snapped back into place.

When he had been younger, he had often gotten into fights he didn't remember. He would come to — out of breath and exhausted — in the aftermath with blood on his hands and moaning bodies spread around him.

He had always hated it.

After getting married, he promised to stop. It had taken years, but eventually he was able to hold his temper. Calm down. Chill out.

But every once in a while, that anger would hit again. He would struggle to keep it from blooming into rage.

Jennifer's story ... the way she still fought to get out from under the abuse she suffered, and the weight of her own poor self-image, was enough to spark the anger. Getting shot ramped it up. The asshole coming onto *his* boat to attack him was gas to flames.

The anger narrowed to the focus of a torch, and the rage built to banish the pain of the cuts on his hand, the burn the bullet had traced in his scalp, and the broken nose.

All that was left was the air filling his lungs. The sound of his heartbeat in his ears. The hate he felt for anybody trying to hurt him or the ones he loved.

As his right hand stopped the asshole's hammer blow, the left one searched through the debris for a weapon. Spikes of distant pain when his fingers closed on something, and Longjohn swung it up to hit the asshole in the face with a cactus.

The skin on his palm was tougher than the skin on the asshole's face, and when he let go, it stuck in his cheek. The asshole screamed and reached for it, but Longjohn clamped his fingers on his wrist and pulled the guy down to put him off balance, then he put everything he had into a left-handed punch that landed right in the center of the cactus hanging from the guy's face.

The asshole squealed in pain as he flew back to land between Longjohn's feet.

Longjohn took a moment for a deep breath before grabbing the leg of an overturned chair to help him up.

When he straightened, he still had the chair in his hands. How convenient.

The asshole rolled over with a groan, and Longjohn brought the chair down on his back. It exploded into kindling, and Longjohn pulled back nothing but a broken dowel. With his weapon mostly destroyed, he had nothing to swing. So he kicked instead.

The asshole flew in a tidy arc with a dramatic explosion of breath to crash into the backside of the counter. The cabinet underneath it tore up with a splintering crack and dumped everything on it into the floor.

Longjohn stepped on a rolling coffee cup, and his foot came out from under him like he was in a cartoon.

He landed flat on his back with an impact that sent a shockwave through his nervous system. His diaphragm seized, and he couldn't get a breath. Blinding white panic as his lungs refused to work, and he clawed at the floor next to him as he sat up.

The asshole's feet churned underneath him as he tried to get up. With his head down as he pushed, he couldn't see Longjohn lift the jagged bit of wood still in his hand over his head.

Longjohn whipped the point of it down into the asshole's neck. It tore out the side in a spray of blood, and the asshole fell back against the uprooted cabinet. He rolled off the side and hit the kitchen floor on his face. Spurting blood arced through the air, and the asshole sucked in a wet breath as he got his feet under him again.

He was in a near sprint by the time he got to the back door. He took it off its hinges on his way out. He slowed to a stumble when he got outside, hitting the railing with his thighs and tumbling over.

The splash as he fell into the ocean made Longjohn laugh, breaking his paralysis. One whooping breath after another, and he laughed until cramps formed in his gut. They tapered into giggles, and he wiped the snot and blood from his nose before lying back down. Just a tiny rest before checking in on Mark and Jennifer.

When he closed his eyes, the rain stopped. That meant it would be nice and quiet for his nap.

Chapter Thirty-One

When Mark limped back out to jump to the dock, the clouds broke to let sunlight through. Like shafts from heaven marking the marina where the good people were.

He threw off the lines toward the bow, but before he could tell Jennifer to do the same toward the stern, she was already there. The choppy water made the boat rub against the bumpers along the boardwalk, but he wasn't worried about damage.

With her help, he got the sewer, water, and shore power disconnected. She worked quickly and took directions well, and soon they were in a rhythm with each other, even though they barely spoke.

When they jumped back on board, the boat had drifted enough that the distance made for a tough landing. His right knee buckled with a knife of pain, but he was able to stay on his feet by grabbing onto Jennifer's shoulder and nearly dragging her down.

They ran inside and stuck in the doorway for a moment like it was part of an old comedy routine. Then they popped through, and he led her to the center hallway and into the front room, where he had his controls set up in a large cabinet by the bank of windows. "It'll be tricky getting out with the storm churning the water up, but we should be alright."

He eased out of his dock to enter the lane that passed the other boats, and he winced in anticipation, but nothing scraped the sides. He tapped his nav screen, then looked back at Jennifer. "Where do your parents live? Where's their house?"

"Key Largo. They'll be there tonight, but soon they'll be going up to Maine."

"Shit," Mark shouted. "We're on the Gulf Coast."

"Reg and I have an apartment on this side. My truck is there. We can dock and drive."

"Sounds good to me."

Mark steered them to where the marina widened into the sea. A few other boats were moving around, but the storm kept them locked down, so he didn't have to worry about traffic. "We'll stay in deeper water to get some flat seas, but it's still gonna be rough."

Blood had trickled down his arm to make it to the heel of his hand. His wheel had become sticky with it.

He keyed in the destination on his screen with his other hand. He'd made similar runs up and down the coast before. A course was already charted. He grabbed her shoulder and pulled her over to the controls to point at the screen. "See that line? Until we're clear, keep the speed the same, and just steer us to stay on that line, okay?"

She took his place at the controls but kept her hands at her side. "What? I don't know how to drive a boat. Or whatever you call it."

"*Drive* is fine. And yes, you do, you just don't know it. I need to pack this thing in my shoulder off so blood doesn't keep dripping off my fingers."

She looked down to see the wheel covered in a slick of blood and took a half step back. Then she looked over at the blood dripping from his hand and gasped in shocked sympathy.

Before she could bend down to help, he gently pushed her back to the controls. "I know where the first-aid is. It won't take long for me to get it. You'll be fine. Do you want a towel?"

She shook her head and grabbed the wheel, her eyes fixed on the screen. "I'm sorry. This is all my fault."

"Damn right it is, lady. You're lucky I don't jump off and swim for shore."

Ow. But when she saw his smile, she laughed with relief. "That's not funny."

Mark turned to go back through the hallway. "It was a little bit funny."

Between the rough water and his limp, he bounced his shoulders off both walls with every step to the kitchen. He made it to the cabinet by the side door and pulled the whole first-aid case off the wall.

"How long will it take?" she shouted.

"About four hours. Depends on conditions."

"St. James has helicopters."

Mark hurried back to the front. "We shouldn't have to worry about 'em. Naval Air Command doesn't like shit like that."

He set the kit down on his captain's chair. Opened it up and wriggled out of his shirt. There was no alcohol. He couldn't remember what he had used it for. He wanted to punch something in his frustration.

Jennifer sucked in a shocked breath. She looked at his bloody shoulder.

"Pretty bad?" he asked.

"It looks awful."

He dropped to his knees and reached across her thighs into the cabinet under the controls. "Excuse me."

"Eww, when you do that, it gapes open."

He pulled out a bottle of vodka. Better than nothing. "Sorry. I'll do better."

"See that you do."

To hear the smile in her voice made the pain more bearable. But that was about to end. He gritted his teeth and tipped the bottle up over his shoulder. As it burned into the gaping wound, a door in the hallway opened.

When he tried to get up, his knee dumped him onto his ass. His teeth clacked together, and the vodka bottle fell from his hand to gurgle its contents across the floor.

Reggie Fallon and three men filed down the hallway. They each held a gun. MP5s for the men. A large silver Desert Eagle .45 for Reg.

"I agree about the helicopters," he said. He turned to one of the men — a wiry African American with a glistening beard. "Take over for her, Dawes."

Dawes motioned with the rifle to step aside. Jennifer lifted her hands up and stepped into the spilled vodka. Her face was empty, like she was moving out of habit. Dawes took the wheel, standing sideways so he could keep Jennifer and Mark in view.

Reg pointed at the ceiling. "You two really fucked me, you know that? It's still salvageable. I mean, I'm gonna have to do some tweaking of the plan. Edit the story a little. But I think I can still get it done. No thanks to Hayes." He lowered his finger to point at Mark. "Piece of advice. Don't hire your friends."

Mark sat up with his hands on the floor behind him to keep him braced. "But you said *we* were friends."

Reg's genuine smile made it clear there was *something* Jennifer had liked about him. "And see where it got me?"

Mark threw his head back in a fake laugh. Shook his head as he pretended to catch his breath. "A broken nose, a bunch of dead employees, and Harbor Patrol on its way."

"Come on, you don't think we're monitoring the radio? There's no Harbor Patrol coming. Besides, they're too busy investigating the explosion at the Sediment Key Beach. Nicely done, by the way."

Mark grinned. "Hey, thanks."

He thought it was a pretty good impression of Brad when Jennifer had given him his cookies back. Her surprised laugh must have meant she thought it was pretty good as well.

Reg narrowed his eyes in confusion. He looked out the front windows. "See if this is funny. We're just gonna keep on keepin' on for now. Up the coast like you two planned. Her truck. Over to Mommy and Daddy's house. Then, I'll make it look like you killed them, and *boom*. We'll actually be a little ahead."

Mark ignored the guns as he got to his hands and knees. He fought to get to his feet without crumbling back to the floor, and when he made it, he spread his hands like a kid finishing a magic trick. "There. Now that I'm on my feet, I can tell you something very important."

Reg's infuriating polite smile became wary. "What's that?"

"There's no fucking way I'm giving up my boat."

Reg leaned back in disbelief. "You may notice, you already *have*." When he rocked back onto his toes, he shot Mark in the right thigh.

The bullet blew flesh and fabric into the air. His knee collapsed, and he fell again. There was no pain. Only a cold numbness. He hit the floor with his lower leg folded underneath him. The back of his head bounced into the vodka with a splat.

Jennifer dropped onto all fours next to his knee. She put her hands over the blood coming out of the wound, but the bullet had passed through the meat so there was an exit wound as well. It would need to be wrapped up if they were going to stop the bleeding.

"Man," Mark whined. "I just stood back up. Now I gotta do it again?"

Reg's face darkened with anger as he watched Jennifer tend to Mark's leg. "No, you can stay down there."

He lunged forward and grabbed a handful of Jennifer's hair. He lifted her to her feet and put his gun under her chin. When the anger drained away to be replaced by the polite smile again, Mark closed his eyes.

He was sure Reg was going to blow her head off, and he couldn't bear to look.

Chapter Thirty-Two

Reg's barrel dug into the skin under her jaw, but his fingers in her hair kept her from pulling away. The usual feeling of shame welled up in her chest. She wanted to look away and apologize, but she held his gaze.

The emotion left his eyes, but his smile remained.

"Do you know how easy it was to track you? Even without the earrings?" He looked at Mark. "I had your number all along, but I didn't know enough about you. I misjudged you. I'm sorry for that."

Mark opened his eyes and waved his words away like they were no big deal. "Don't worry about it."

"But now I know everything about you. Where you went to school. How long you served. How you got injured. It doesn't help me set you up, but it helps me know you better. You're a drunk. Hanging onto them glory days, only they weren't all that glorious, were they? But I also found out where you lived. The location of this boat."

He pulled her hair, forcing her head back until she looked at the ceiling. He put the gun over her heart, jabbing the barrel into her breast. "And here you were together. But I should have known. You stared at another man's wife. Right in front of him."

"You were the one that dressed her in pink dental floss."

"Is that what she told you? My man, you have no idea how many have fallen for her lies. For that *poor little ol' me* act. But I don't blame you. I fell for it too."

He transferred his hand from her hair to her throat. He drove her back, and her toes barely touched the floor. He rammed her into the wall, and she grabbed his wrist.

"Stay on the floor!" one of the men shouted. Mark must have tried to save her? While he was bleeding on the floor, he still thought about her?

She wondered for the thousandth time what it was about Reg that had made her fall in love with him, or whatever she had convinced her love was supposed to feel like. How had she been blind to the absolute douche he really was?

Maybe it was to make her father happy. *He* liked Reg. Her *mother* liked him, too. Or maybe it was her need to make them proud of her that made her put their feelings above hers.

Like she always did.

She looked into Reg's eyes and dropped her hands. Her head pounded from the impact, and her heartbeat echoed in her ears from the pressure of his chokehold, but she smiled. As sweet and pleased as she could manage.

He stepped back like he was offended. Dropped his hand and looked away.

"Dawes," he said. "Stay the course. Williams, take her to one of the rooms back there and tie her up. Be *rough*. Green, stay with me and get on the radio. Give the boat our course, and tell 'em to meet us en route. I'm gonna hang out with my new friend here for a while."

"What are you going to do?" Jennifer asked.

"I'm going to ask your boyfriend some questions. Then I'm going to kill him."

～

LONGJOHN SNAPPED awake with a deep inhale that led to a coughing fit. He worked his bulk over to his knees to spit bloody phlegm onto the floor. He reached for the counter to pull himself to his feet, but it wasn't there. He looked over to see the cabinet crumbled into scrap.

Chairs on their sides. The table overturned. Blood and glass everywhere.

He stood up and looked out the windows, shielding his eyes from the bright sunlight. It had been as dark as night just a few minutes ago. He could see boats trolling around the marina. People on the boardwalks, checking for damage.

Only a few people close to his end, since his were the only two boats docked by the seawall, but he figured they'd be coming soon enough. He had no idea how long he had been out, but it was too long, for sure. He needed to get moving. He washed his hands, but when a couple of the cuts on his left hand wouldn't stop bleeding, he wadded a paper towel up with a growl and stalked to the back door. Just as he stepped through the debris, the main electric bypass switch *thunked* closed, and the lights came back on. It looked like shore power was back on.

Right when he didn't need it.

He grumbled under his breath as he walked out onto his rear deck. A bloody trail led to the water. He stood at the railing and looked over. Just past his reflection on the bobbing surface was a body. The asshole that had attacked him.

Longjohn's guts felt full of fire. His anger was growing into a crescendo of rage. Unstoppable emotion that would lead him to do something stupid. Before their divorce, Janie had said it would get him killed one day.

"Maybe it's today," he said.

He moved to the deck on the port side to get to the opening in the dock railing, but before he stepped over, he saw a rifle sitting on the tool ledge. Black and menacing and so enticing. He rushed through and got down on his knees to reach under the overhang of the boardwalk, and pulled the rifle up.

An AR-15. Standard attachments. Sling adjusted for someday much shorter. He wondered if Jennifer had put it there. He decided to believe she had. It made him feel good to use a rifle she had used.

He checked the magazine and the breech with an approving nod and stood up with the gun pointed at the ground.

"Whoa," a voice said. "I don't think you can just walk around with that thing like that."

Longjohn turned to see Carl Camber, Retired Air Force. A skinny old man with ears the size of maple leaves. He loved nothing more than boring somebody with the same stories over a can of Busch Light. Carl recoiled in alarm when he saw Longjohn's face.

"Then go call Harbor Patrol," Longjohn said.

He moved along the line to his other boat, a Ranger Z519. He told everybody it was a fishing boat, but with a two hundred and twenty-five horsepower Mercury engine in it, he mostly used it to give people whiplash.

"What the hell happened to you, Johnnie? And what happened to your boat?"

Longjohn jumped aboard the Ranger and stowed the

rifle next to the controls. He ignored Carl's question as he threw off the lines and pushed away from the dock.

"Was it the storm? I thought I heard something like glass breaking. Was that your generator that was backfiring? I swear, I ain't never seen anything like the weather we had today."

Longjohn did a quick pre-launch check before sitting in his seat. His reflection in the small windscreen looked like a car crash victim stared back at him.

"I remember one time we was over in Sugarloaf, and a wind come up like I'd never seen. Blew the RV right off its jacks."

Longjohn paused before turning the key. "Carl, can you shut up for a goddamned second?"

Carl's mouth snapped closed.

"Some men tried to kill me and Mark Adler. And the lady he's with—"

"Mark's got a lady?"

"*And the lady he's with* is in danger. On their way up to Key Largo, and I'm gonna chase 'em down. So, *please*, call the Harbor Patrol. Tell 'em I have a gun and I'm going crazy. I don't really give a fuck what you tell them, just send 'em after me, okay?"

Carl blinked slowly before nodding his head. "Sure, I can do that. Right now?"

Longjohn dropped his head in defeat. "Yes, right now."

He turned away before Carl could ask another question. When the Mercury barked off, it sounded like a shotgun behind him. A sound that always made him smile.

Without waiting for it to warm up, he ripped away from his dock to thread out of the marina. Breaking the NO WAKE rule would piss a lot of people off. The Harbor Patrol phones would be ringing off the hook.

Chapter Thirty-Three

Mark slid over to lean against the cabinet under the control console. It was supposed to have charts and gear in it, but he had turned it into a liquor cabinet. Bottles and glasses held with bungee cords.

And a gun for when he was at the wheel, looking at the sunset and contemplating suicide. Right behind the bottle of Evan Williams.

Dawes skated back to keep distance between them, splitting his attention between the GPS screen and Mark's position. Mark waved at him with a pained expression he hoped looked like he didn't want to start any trouble.

The initial burst of blood from the gunshot wound had slowed to a trickle. Maybe it was shock or old scar tissue. Either way, Mark had to take advantage of it. There was one man steering. Another chilling behind Reg with a gun trained casually on the floor in front of Mark. Then there was the man himself.

As sun blazed through the port side windows, Reg squinted in annoyance. He squatted down in front of Mark. "Who else have you talked to on the way to here?"

Mark pretended to have trouble thinking. "Nobody."

"So just the old man in the houseboat Lewis and Hayes boarded?"

"Did they kill him?"

Reg sighed and looked away. "I'm not gonna lie. We haven't heard from any of 'em."

Mark closed his eyes. He refused to believe Longjohn was dead, but if he was, it was easy to believe he had killed the last man on his way out. Mark forced a smile. "I killed one of 'em. Cut his throat and let him sink to the bottom."

"You did?"

Mark opened his eyes to see Reg looking at him with genuine pride. For a split second he felt good about impressing him. "Yeah, it was easy. When you take over St. James, you should invest in better training."

Reg's face transitioned from pride to rage so quickly, Mark tucked his chin to his chest in preparation for the coming blow. He wondered if Jennifer had to do something similar when she talked to him.

Reg swiped at his head with the barrel of the gun. Mark took most of it but turned into it to lessen the impact. He flopped like a soccer star, throwing himself to the side and crashing into the cabinet to scatter bottles and glasses in a distracting clatter.

As he pretended to slip and slide on the rolling glass, he curled into the cabinet and grabbed the gun. He stuffed it into the front of his waistband and collapsed. Alcohol-coated glass shards burned as they jabbed into the skin of his chest and cheek.

Dawes grabbed him by the shoulders and dragged him away. He threw Mark down and looked back at the mess on the floor. He gingerly picked a spot in the middle of it that kept the controls in reach and took the wheel again.

Reg shielded his eyes from the glare and scanned the

ocean through the front windows. "I think I see our boat, boys."

He shifted to the side to get a better view, putting himself between Mark and Green, Reg's other man. Mark reached under his shirt and grabbed the pistol. His blood-slicked hands made him bobble the pull, but he still got it out before anybody could react, only his aim was off.

Instead of hitting him in the head, the bullet plowed through Reg's shoulder. He flew back into Green's arms, and Mark leaned over to shoot Dawes up into the crotch. When he bent over with a liquid squeal, Mark shot him in the face and dodged away to keep the body from falling on top of him, but Dawes fell quicker than Mark's injured leg would let him move. He clipped Mark's elbow, and the gun flew from his hand.

Reg slapped his fingers over his wound as Green struggled to get from under the weight of his body pressing him into the bulkhead. He freed his rifle and pushed away from the wall.

Mark's gun was too far away, and Dawes had died on his, so Mark abandoned them both in favor of a physical attack. He pulled himself up using the wheel and steadied himself on his good leg. He threw himself forward in an awkward dive and crashed into Reg's chest, driving both men back into the wall again.

Green fired off a shot that shattered a front window. Mark reached past Reg's head and grabbed Green by the throat. He lifted his legs to hang all his weight from his grip, bringing the two men down on top of him. Mark let go to hit Reg in the side of the neck with an elbow before hitting Green's wrist with a hammer fist. When he brought the same fist up to paste one across Green's nose, the gun fell from his dazed fingers, and Mark twisted under their combined weight to grab it.

Mark's fingers were touching the handgrip when Reg swatted it away. He brought his pistol up toward Mark's head, but Mark hit him in the throat with a weak shot of his left hand. Enough to make Reg rear back, and Mark bucked his hips to make enough room to scoot out from under him.

Reg coughed and gagged behind him as Mark crawled toward the rifle. Green snarled and jumped over Reg's legs. Mark took a deep breath and braced for impact. When Green landed on his back, he felt the pop of several vertebrae adjusting in his spine.

An arm snaked around Mark's throat, but he got a hand up in time to keep enough space in the hold to breathe. Green pulled to bend him into a painful backward arch, his rasping hiss in Mark's ear like a deflating tire.

Mark pushed his head as far forward as he could. He let go of Green's arm just as he slammed his head back into the man's face. The pressure around his neck disappeared, and the weight rolled off his back.

Mark stretched forward to grab a bottle of Rittenhouse Rye rolling by and scrambled into a spin that left him on his knees with his back to the front windows. Reg coughed into his hand like he was trying to be polite, but he pulled the pistol around to point it at Mark, squinting up at him from under his eyebrows.

Mark swung the bottle up from the floor to shatter against Reg's fingers. Glass and whiskey flew into the air in a sparkling cascade. The gun spun into the hallway. Reg stumbled back and cradled his hand into his gut, covering it with his other hand and curling over with his teeth gritted in pain.

Green leaned against the wall with his head down as blood dripped from his split lips. He caught a large shard that was headed for his face with one hand and flung it behind him.

Reg stepped back to lean against the corner leading into the hallway. Thin red ropes squeezed through his fingers and sagged to the floor between his feet.

Mark took a few deep breaths before putting his good foot out to plant his weight on it. Pushing against his knee with both hands, he grunted to his feet.

He looked from Reg to Green and back. "It's like sitting at a four-way stop with dudes that just got their license. I can't stand up much longer, so somebody better do something."

Green straightened and wiped his hand on his shirt.

Reg looked down the hall like he was thinking of running to the other side of the boat. He pointed at the ceiling. "Let's do it, then."

Mark put everything he had into his good leg to jump forward, but Reg stayed put. Green rushed out to meet him instead.

Chapter Thirty-Four

Drake led the way past the Harbormaster's office. Power had come back on just a few minutes after the rain had stopped. He heard plenty of jokes about the *perfect timing*, but whatever. He and August had to patrol no matter what.

They passed the small bar that already smelled like heating grease. He was looking forward to having a few cold ones there tonight. Maybe Mark and that cute number he was with would come by.

The radio had been crackling with reports nonstop, and he could hear the phone ringing in the office. One in particular they had to investigate was a NO WAKE violation with dangerous operation. The exact kind of thing some of these bored retirees liked to complain about.

That thought wasn't fair. He hoped to be one of those guys one day.

"I'm not kidding," he said. "Adler and Longjohn had a fish fry the other day that was off the chain."

August's snort of laughter sounded bored. "Off the chain, huh?"

"Yeah, it just sounds like they like to party, you know?"

"It sounds like they like to drink."

Drake shrugged. "Whatever. I doubt it'll be that big a thing."

August pointed to a withered man in an Air Force ball cap. "Is that Carl?"

"Yup."

"What's he want?"

"Probably one of the ones that called in. Or he has something else he wants to report. Like too much sun or everything's too wet."

August laughed and stepped in front of Drake to intercept the old man. "We've heard about the NO WAKE, Carl. We're on it."

The old man waved his hands in front of his face. "No, no. That's not what I want to report. Well ... it *is*, but I need to tell you something else."

"Can it wait until we check this out first? We gotta go check out a possible theft."

Carl furrowed his brow in confusion. "I thought it was a NO WAKE violation."

"Among other things, but it looked like Longjohn's boat."

"It was. I saw him take off."

August stopped to look back at Drake with raised eyebrows. He turned back and grabbed Carl's shoulder. "You saw him take off. It was Longjohn?"

"Yeah, and he told me to tell you somebody tried to kill him and Mark Adler, and the young woman he was with. Mark, not Longjohn. He hasn't brought a lady here for years. You know, he used to—"

August held his finger up, and Carl stopped talking to focus on it like he was being hypnotized. "Longjohn said somebody was trying to kill him?"

"That's right," Carl said. "And he had blood all over him. Hands and face cut up pretty good. He says to tell you he has a gun and he's gone crazy. And there's a body in the water behind his boat."

Drake jumped forward in surprise. "He fucking said what?"

August pushed Carl aside and drew his SIG Sauer M17 pistol. He motioned for Drake to follow. Drake dropped into a fast crouch and drew his own pistol. He heard August calling it in on his comm. Calm and quiet, even though his eyes were wide with shock and excitement.

Drake knew how he felt. Nothing ever happened here except drunken disputes and dumping violations. Open fires or generators running after quiet hours.

He followed August down the boardwalk to Longjohn's houseboat. He walked to the stern while August stepped through the railing to the deck. Drake looked down to see the body Carl had mentioned. It wouldn't be there long if they didn't get it out of there. Something would come along and eat it.

He glanced over next door, and Longjohn's Ranger was gone.

"Drake!" August motioned him to join him at the side door.

Drake moved back along the dock. He waved Carl back. "Get outta here. Jesus."

Carl nodded with an amused smile, but he didn't budge. Drake had never seen dudes that didn't give a fuck anymore like old retired service members.

He joined August at the door, and they breached as a two-man team to clear the boat before Harbor Patrol arrived.

"It looks like somebody went to war on this thing,"

August said. "How much blood *is* that? Two people? Three?"

"A lot of weapons on board, too. Longjohn's gonna get in trouble, for sure. Lose his spot, probably."

"If he's still alive."

August pointed at the back door. "It looked like somebody got thrown through that bitch."

"Probably the dead guy floating around out there."

"So there *is* a body like Carl said?" August shook his head. "If they go out there to get this guy, I don't think I want to be there. I always thought that old man was a badass, but I didn't know he was such a fucking savage." He pointed at the deck. "Is that a bloody cactus?"

"So somebody tried to kill him and Mark Adler, and he got pissed? Like some Revenant shit?"

August picked his way through the broken glass and looked out the window to where Adler's boat would have been. "Fuck, he's gone. Adler's *gone.*"

"So, is Longjohn after him, or the ones that tried to kill him? Or does Carl have it wrong, and Adler is the one tried to kill him?"

August holstered his pistol. "I don't know. Only that I wouldn't want to be either one of them when Longjohn gets there."

Drake went outside to wait for Harbor Patrol.

August joined him at the railing. "I tell you what," he said. "I really want to see how this turns out."

"I'm not so sure."

"Why?"

Drake looked out over the bustling marina. "I don't know. I just like him. I don't want anything to happen to him."

"Yeah well, sometimes things happen. Even to people we like."

"That's why I don't want to know."

August slapped him on the shoulder in sympathy on his way by.

Chapter Thirty-Five

Williams shouldered the door open and threw Jennifer on the bed. Her head smacked off the padded headboard. Her teeth closed on her tongue, and she rolled over to spit blood onto the floor as he entered to stand over her.

She remembered him from the trip to Islamorada, where he'd picked them up at her parents' house. He had driven the limo. So polite and respectful when he had offered his hand to help her inside.

A sneering grin replaced the courtesy, and he dropped down to plant his knee on the back of her neck.

"Reg says he wants to teach you a lesson before he kills you. He says you take it pretty good, too." He slid his knee off and bent forward to speak close to her ear. "We're gonna make it look like the Navy boy raped you. Maybe the same for your mom."

Jennifer bit back the frightened wail that threatened to rise into her throat. She gritted her teeth and held her breath instead. Her vision turned red. White spots danced in front of her eyes.

Williams straightened to put one foot up on the

mattress. She looked up at him as he put his hands on his hips with a smug smile. He lifted an eyebrow and stared into her eyes.

A gunshot shattered the uncomfortable moment of poise, and Williams leaned back with his face drawing down in concern. He lifted his foot to step down, and Jennifer sprang up to punch him in the balls.

His foot slipped off as he bent over to cup his hands over his crotch. His MP5 swung on the sling. Jennifer went for it, but he spun away, throwing his hand out to block her from following.

She grabbed his wrist with both hands and swung her leg up from the bed to graze the top of his head and down his face. She dug her heel into his chin and pushed him back to land on the bed. She kicked her other leg up to lock her ankles together, and she leaned back in an armbar.

Don had put her in Jiu Jitsu when she turned eighteen. She had rolled with men larger and stronger than her for years, but she never got sick of getting her ass kicked, because she got better every day.

A man off his guard taken by surprise was still danger-ous, so she had learned to strike first, as hard as she could.

Her weight pulled Williams half out of the bed, and the tops of her shoulders hit the floor a moment before the back of her head made contact. She pushed her hips into his elbow and straightened his arm with a scream of effort that wasn't loud enough to cover up the sound of the joint tearing apart. Like a head of lettuce splitting in half.

He bucked off the bed, and his rifle bounced into the hallway. Jennifer let go and rolled forward to crawl over him to get the weapon, but a looping left hand coming up from his hip hit her under her right ear, and she collapsed onto his face as heat radiated down into her neck.

He worked his good arm under her and pushed her over his head. The corner of the bed dug into her back as he sat up and rotated to face the door. She flopped over to get her feet into position — one braced, and one swinging — and kicked him in the face. It felt like her shin broke against his cheekbone.

Williams fell back with both arms straight out to the side. His eyes focused several feet past the ceiling. Jennifer didn't feel like it was enough, so she got to her feet to stand over him. She fell to plant her knees on his groin.

He folded up like he had been spring loaded, falling to the side with a broken wheeze.

Jennifer took a moment to catch her breath before turning around to lunge for the gun in the hallway, but Williams grabbed her ankle.

His face burned red with pain and anger, and he fell on top of her to claw along her body like he was climbing a hill.

"You fucking bitch," he gasped.

A knee in the center of her back, and he pulled her hair, bending her neck until it creaked. She was getting sick of people using her long hair against her.

His other hand swooped down to punch her in the side of the head. Then he let her hair go so the rebound of her contracted muscles would slam her face into the floor. A nice one-two.

She got up to sway on her knees. Were the walls moving, or was it her? Her guts tightened with a cramp. She swallowed to keep the nausea down and pushed to her feet.

Williams staggered the last step to the hallway where he bent down, holding the edge of the door to grab the gun. Jennifer looked at the inverted V of his crotch and shrugged. It hadn't been as successful as she had wanted the first two times, so why not a third?

She lined up and jumped back to give her room before swinging her toes into his balls so hard, something popped in her ankle.

Williams shot forward to hit the opposite wall nose first. A smear of blood followed him down, and he landed on his side to curl up in a choking ball.

Jennifer hopped to the bed with a squeal of pain. She brought her foot up to hold her ankle, rocking back and forth as she rubbed it.

~

MARK DUCKED under Green's wild hook. He fired a left into Green's liver, but he couldn't push off his bad leg enough to make it effective. Green's breath exploded out, but it didn't stop him from bringing an overhand left down into the side of Mark's face.

Mark dropped to the floor like he was about to do a pushup. Green helped him with his first rep with a kick to the ribs, flipping him over onto his back. Mark could barely get any air, but he was able to get his good leg up when Green hopped forward to drop on top of him.

Mark's foot hit in the center of Green's chest, and Green's weight pushed his knee back almost to his own shoulder. Green drew back a fist and Mark drove through his heel to push Green back toward the hallway. He tried grabbing the walls to stop his momentum, but his hands scraped down the sides as he continued to stumble back.

Williams flew out of the bedroom door to hit the wall with his face. He collapsed in a ball, and Green caught him with his heels to fall backward. Eyes wide and arms flailing, he tumbled straight back. His head cracked off the floor with the sound of a lofted bowling ball.

Mark rolled over to get on all fours. He sat with his head down until he could get a deep breath against the pain down his side. Finally, he got to his feet to look out the window. The boat Reg had used earlier was only a few hundred yards away. Soon, it would be close enough for the men to board him.

Mark hobbled over to the controls. A growl behind him made him turn around in confusion. He had forgotten about Reg.

He opened his mouth to call himself a *dumbass*, but Reg got to him first. He hit Mark just above his waistband in a tackle that lifted him into the air. His lower back crashed into the controls, and they tumbled over to crash onto the floor. The top of Mark's head scraped down the other side of the cabinet, and he ended up lying on top of Reg like they were sharing the same sleeping bag.

Blood dripped from his scalp to land in Reg's face. Reg snarled with disgust and pushed Mark away as he rolled in the opposite direction. Reg jumped to his feet. Mark followed much slower. He grabbed the edge of the window frame to brace as the boat accelerated. They must have kicked up the throttle when they went over.

Mark glanced out the window. They were gonna meet the other boat much sooner than he'd thought.

He looked back at Reg. "Got anybody that can steer for a while?"

Reg smiled and pointed at the ceiling. "When they get here, there will be plenty of men for all *kinds* of things."

Mark grinned like it was the best news he'd ever heard. "Great, then I don't have anything to worry about."

Reg flung blood from his mangled hand to the floor.

He tensed to rush forward, but Mark pulled himself by the window frame and jumped through to the outer deck.

When Reg ran into the wall with a curse, Mark laughed so hard his abs cramped. He turned his head to the side in case he threw up.

Reg leaned through the window with a growl. He looked at the boat approaching along the side, and he smiled before ducking back in. He slammed the throttle down to shut the engine off and walked to the hallway. He turned back to the window, then he stepped sideways to stand in front of the door with a smile.

Mark got to his knees, knowing his bad leg would never let him get on his feet.

Chapter Thirty-Six

Roger Pearl stood at the forward railing of the boat with one foot up on the bulkhead. He held his MP5 in front of him and scanned the horizon as they approached the houseboat. He loved this duty because it made him feel like a pirate.

Any time he got to do anything on the water, he jumped at the chance. Thank God his job was based in the Florida Keys. He got to do tons of security on boats, and every time, the only thing he felt was missing was a sword and some cannons.

Maybe an eye patch.

Reg had wanted him to grab three other guys for the op, but there had only been two available. Sykes and Maynard. The only other ones left were St. James regulars. He didn't think Reg wanted any of them. They were too loyal to the old man.

He signaled to Sykes by pointing to the houseboat they were heading toward. He knew Sykes could see just fine, but pointing to it made him feel like the captain pointing out a course. He wanted to shout, "Land ho!"

He covered his giggle with the back of his hand.

They were only a handful of yards away, but it looked like the houseboat had sped up. It would pass them right by if they weren't careful. He twirled his finger in the air, but Sykes was already cutting into a turn that would bring them alongside. When a man jumped through the forward window to land on his side on the front deck, Pearl was sure he had been grinning like a madman. Reg poked his head out behind him with a snarl. Stuck his leg through to climb out, then ducked back inside.

Pearl looked back at Sykes, his arms spreading in an incredulous question, but he didn't get a chance to ask it.

A speedboat hidden by the houseboat's bulk knifed through the water like an arrow. He heard the scream of the engine above the wind. Saw a grin on the pilot's face as manic as the guy who had jumped out of the houseboat window.

His long white hair and beard streamed back behind him. Like a pirate riding the waves toward battle.

Pearl stepped back to shout a warning but saw it was too late. The speedboat was going to hit them.

LONGJOHN SKIMMED over the houseboat's wake, but every time he hit the peak of a wave, the impact raced up his spine into his teeth. Good thing they were all fake.

The way he'd torn out of the marina, he wouldn't be surprised if Harbor Patrol was only a few minutes behind him. He resisted the urge to look back to see if they had appeared yet. Instead, he kept his gaze fixed on the houseboat.

He looked along the edge of it to see another boat getting close. He couldn't go any faster, so he held on, nudging the steering to bring him alongside the houseboat without exposing himself.

The other boat swung around, and Longjohn saw the men on board. Matching clothes and weapons. Bad guys.

The one at the front railing stood like Captain Morgan. Longjohn aimed right for him.

Just before he pulled level with the rear of Mark's houseboat, he hit the neutral button and dropped down to brace against the lower bulkhead under the controls. He hugged the AR-15 to his chest like it was a teddy bear and he was ready for bed.

He didn't get to snuggle in for the night. Though, it occurred to him that he might not wake up.

His Ranger hit the other boat at about fifty knots.

A roaring crush of metal and fiberglass, and the bulkhead he pressed against split from the pressure of it stopping his weight. The Ranger cut through most of the other boat to hang up in the port side hull.

His motor screamed at six thousand RPMs. The other boat's engine chugged along as it was, and the boat's previous wide turn became a slow spiral that scraped against the houseboat with every lazy circle.

Longjohn got up, but the spin made him fall back down again. He felt drunk as he tried and failed to get to his feet three more times.

He got to his knees and grabbed a jagged rip of fiberglass for support. Captain Morgan was gone. Longjohn looked for him on the boat, but most of the bow was gone. The pilot was draped over the controls, with blood dribbling out of his mouth. He moaned as he straightened. When he saw Longjohn, his eyes widened as he reached for the MP5 dangling by its sling.

Longjohn shot him twice in the chest. Stalked over after the body fell to the deck and put another in his head to be sure. Black smoke billowed around him to burn his eyes and sting his throat.

He staggered to the railing and held on to steady himself while he surveyed the water. Oil and fuel formed a slick on top. His engine chugged as it slowed. Picked back up to roar like he had opened it up to full throttle.

Sparks spit out from under the cover.

The spiral carried the boats back around in another circle, and Longjohn saw the captain floundering in the water. He looked like his only problem was he didn't know how to swim. Longjohn shot him in the neck and face. Waited for him to sputter under the surface before looking for the third man.

His engine squealed with seizing metal. More sparks and thick greasy smoke. The engine on Captain Morgan's boat choked off with a backfire, and the spin picked up to send Longjohn stumbling away from the center.

He grabbed the rail to stay on board. Looked down into the eyes of the man he had been looking for. Half in the water, his face was a smear of gore.

He pointed his gun at Longjohn's chest.

Longjohn threw himself back as he dumped the rest of his magazine in the man's direction.

Burning pain in his shoulder and along his ribs. The back of his knees hit the opposite rail, and he tipped backward into the water.

He plunged under the surface, and the world became a blur of light and color. The engine sounded like the moan of a whale underwater. Longjohn rolled over to reach away from the boats, kicking off to swim toward the houseboat.

He rose into the waves and looked back between strokes. The struggling engine of his Ranger exploded. A crest of black smoke and debris lifted into the air on a cushion of roiling flames. The heat puckered the skin on the back of his neck as he threw himself away.

He felt his hand slap the hull of Mark's houseboat, but there was nothing to grab onto. He couldn't stay under much longer, but it was too hot above. He thought about his grandkids. Each of their faces flashed into his mind as he dove to swim under the keel to put the houseboat between him and the flames. His vision became red. Rage or blood, he couldn't tell. Soon, the red became black, but he still felt his legs kick as he reached for any handhold he could find.

Chapter Thirty-Seven

Jennifer reached for the gun, but a shadow fell across her. She drew back in alarm to see a man backpedaling down the hall like he was slipping on ice. He fell down on top of Williams and his head hit the floor with a sickening thud.

She winced back and covered her mouth with both hands. When the guy sat up with his eyelids fluttering, she dropped her hands in shock. She was sure hitting his head on the floor like that would have at least knocked him out.

The guy rocked off Williams to get to his knees, but Jennifer wasn't going to let him get to his feet. She snapped a kick into the center of his face. He fell back on top of Williams. His nose was a swollen knot of blood.

Jennifer hopped back into the room on her left foot, pain shooting up from her ankle. She slammed into the wall and dropped her foot to see if it would support her weight.

The joint felt hot and unstable, but it held. She straightened up and got ready to run, but the sound of a collision outside sent her into a frightened crouch. She expected to see a train rush through the room.

She jumped up and looked out the corner window. A black boat shaped like a dagger was in the center of a crater of destruction in a different boat. The combined mass spun in a slow circle, spitting black smoke into a spiral.

In the window's reflection, she saw the guy getting up behind her. She slumped in disbelief. How could he even be moving right now?

As she turned away, gunshots cracked outside. She looked back over her shoulder. A large man with wild white hair — *LONGJOHN* — shot a man getting up from behind the controls. Jennifer couldn't see him clearly, but he looked like one of Reg's friends.

The boats spun away, blocking her view with smoke. When she focused back on the doorway, the guy she had kicked in the face was on his feet. He held on to the door jamb with his head down. She couldn't afford to let him recover.

She screamed as she flew at him to hit him in the chest with a tackle that drove him back into the opposite wall. The paneling split apart under the impact, forming a crater that held them both up. Jennifer pushed away. Paused to stomp on Williams' face before dropping down to finally get the gun he had dropped.

When she pushed up from the floor, her right ankle twisted, dumping her back into the bedroom.

She landed on her tailbone, and her head snapped down, bashing her face into the rifle stock. She fell back as Mr. Indestructible crawled out of the hole in the wall.

Jennifer wiggled back to brace herself against the bed. Shot him in the chest twice. When he collapsed to fall onto her knees, she leaned her head back on the mattress to get a breath.

Movement against her legs made her sit back up

straight. "You gotta be kidding me!" she shouted. But it wasn't Mr. Indestructible. It was Williams — the runner-up for the title — wriggling out from under the body.

She aimed without thinking. Squeezed the trigger in reflex. Another man dead.

She closed her eyes. This is what Reg had made her. Not just a woman willing to sell her soul for acceptance. Not just a woman unable to see who she truly *was* without his guidance. But a woman forced to kill. Always asking permission to be anything more than an accessory — and now fighting to discover if she was even worth knowing.

She threw the rifle aside and covered her face to weep into her hands. The weight of the dead man on her legs was like rising water.

An explosion rocked the boat, and roaring flames brought back to her mind the sound of the rain from the earlier storm. She could barely spare any worry for Longjohn or Mark. She just wanted out.

In spite of the pain in her ankle, Jennifer kicked until her legs were free. She used the bed as support to get to her feet. Used her shirt to wipe her eyes and nose.

She would never let herself be in this position again. From this point on, she would choose. *She* would be the one to say what she wore and where she went. Who she loved.

She picked up the gun again. Checked it for ammo and lifted it into position. This was going to be the last time she held one.

She stepped over the bodies into the hallway to face the broken windows in the front of the boat. Smoke blew past the men outside. Jennifer moved to join them.

This was the last time she was going to kill.

~

REG STEPPED through the door with his pistol in front of him. He must have grabbed it off the floor when he slowed the boat. Perfect.

Mark reached behind him and felt the aluminum leg of a folding chair. It was as good as anything. He whipped around like he was throwing an ax. The chair tumbled through the air to hit Reg's arm as he passed all the way through the door.

The gun fell away to land under a plastic table. The folding chair flew out into the water.

Reg snarled as he bent over to tuck both hands against his stomach. One bleeding from a bottle, the other broken from a chair. It was a start.

Mark sat back on his heels, waiting for Reg to come for him or go for the gun. His knees screamed in agony, but it was better than standing.

Reg stood up with a deep breath, but the men on the boat coming alongside shouted and pointed to the rear of the houseboat. At least, two of them did. The man standing at the railing flapped his arms like he was trying to take flight.

Reg looked over in annoyance right as a speedboat appeared. Longjohn's Ranger, and it was on a collision course.

Mark threw himself to the side and covered his head. The sound of the crash was like a deep-sea monster had surfaced to bite a boat in half. Longjohn's engine screamed at its limit as the other boat's chugged along like usual.

Mark peeked out between his hands in time to see Longjohn jump into the boat with the grace and balance of a much smaller and younger man. He had a rifle held ready. Mark left him to his hunt and faced Reg again.

Reg looked at the two boats spinning in a do-si-do, his face slack with disbelief. He flinched back from gunfire before looking at Mark. His face clouded with anger, and he charged across the deck.

He must have forgotten about his gun.

Before Mark could get out of the way, Reg threw a knee that hit him in the shoulder, knocking him flat. Mark curled up as Reg fell on him. He covered his face in a loose guard, and Reg pulled his right hand back before reconsidering. Blood poured from the vodka bottle slashes.

He lowered it to his side and raised his other hand. Disjointed fingers and misshapen knuckles. He sagged in disappointment. He had no fists to hit with.

Mark opened his guard. "I'm getting pretty tired. How much more of this are we gonna do?"

Reg snarled and lifted both hands anyway, but just as he tensed to bring them down, Longjohn's boat exploded.

Reg's face lit with orange fire, and the blast tore him off of Mark's chest. Heat and burning debris flashed by, and Mark covered his face, feeling the skin on his hands and shoulders burn. Visions of the *Northville* flitted into his mind, but instead of spreading into his waking awareness, they dropped back down into his memory.

They no longer had control.

He rolled away from the railing and across the deck, running into Reg's legs. He looked up to see Reg staring at him with raw hatred. His pistol was right next to his knee. He picked it up with his bloody hand, grimacing in pain as the cuts pulled open, dripping blood as he stood.

Mark crabbed away, but there was nowhere to go. Reg blocked the exit into the water on the houseboat's starboard side. Longjohn's burning boat was off the port side. Back inside? Off the bow where Reg would have a shot anyway?

Mark held his hands up. When Jennifer stepped out onto the deck with an MP5 leveled at Reg's head, Mark let his hands drop back down. He lowered straight onto his back.

"Reg! Stop!" Jennifer shouted.

Reg's snarl morphed into a joyful smile as he looked up at her. He kept his pistol pointed at Mark. "I'm glad you made it. I always said you were tough."

"No, you didn't. You *never* said that."

"Babe, I said it all the time. To anybody that would listen. You were the—"

"Shut up! Just … stop."

Reg looked back at Mark over the barrel of his gun. "She was always so much better than she believed she could be. So self-conscious. If only she loved herself as much as we all do."

"That's bullshit. You *never* loved me. You loved the idea of me. Of *having* me. And now I don't matter to you anymore.

Mark sighed. "For him to no longer love you, he would've had to love you before."

Reg leaned forward with his face burning red as he spat, "Shut the fuck up!" The gun trembled. Blood trickled out between his gripping fingers.

"But did you?" Jennifer asked.

"Did I what?"

"Did you ever love me?"

Reg smiled, but his gaze stayed fixed on Mark. "No. Like you said, I loved the *idea* of you. And what a bad idea you turned out to be."

Mark laughed. "You are an idiot if you don't see it."

Reg drew back in confusion. "See what?"

"She's trying to come up with a reason not to kill you, because she's a far better person than you will ever know."

Reg closed his eyes. He steadied the gun on his other wrist.

"Don't," Jennifer said. "Please, Reg. Don't."

"Is that the sound of the Harbor Patrol I hear?" Reg said.

Mark raised his head. The sound of distant boats. The hum of an approaching helicopter. He dropped his head back to the deck with a smile.

Reg opened his eyes. "Do I want *them* to kill me, or do I want her to do it?"

"You don't deserve either," Mark said.

"Don't make me," Jennifer whispered. "Mark saved me, but he didn't *save* me. If I have to, I'll do it myself."

"Good girl," Reg said. He winked at Mark before spinning to point the gun at Jennifer. She skipped back a single step before opening fire. Reg danced to the beat of three shots to his chest.

He fell back, dead.

Jennifer slid down to her knees. She threw the rifle to the side and wept into her hands. Mark wanted to go to her, but his body wouldn't respond. He was tired and in pain. Besides, she needed to be alone.

When she got up and shuffled over to him, he looked at her in surprise. Like when they had escaped the sailboat, she dropped onto his chest. She cried while he stroked her hair as the sound of the engines got louder.

"Hey, hey," Longjohn said.

Mark craned his neck up to see his friend climb over the railing to drop onto the deck with a groan. He looked like Mark imagined Jonah must have looked like after the whale puked him up on the beach.

Jennifer jumped up with a squeal of glee. She hobbled over to give Longjohn a hug.

The spot where she had been on Mark's chest was suddenly cold.

Chapter Thirty-Eight

THREE WEEKS LATER

ONCE IN CUSTODY, Mark had fallen asleep. He barley remembered being transferred to the infirmary, but after eighteen hours, he had finally woken up in restraints.

MP's standing outside the observation window.

His mouth felt like he had licked a long-haired dog. His nose felt raw where the oxygen tube canula rested. Fire raced along his nerves from head to toe, but his knee was a sickening ball of pounding agony.

It was so much like waking up after the *Northville*. The pain and disorientation. Then the chains of the cuffs around his wrist rattled, and he sighed in relief. He had fallen back asleep before drawing a fresh breath.

The next time he woke up, there were no restraints and no guards. Just the incessant noise of the monitors, and the ache of the IV line in the back of his hand.

In some ways, the recovery was much harder than the

Northville. He was older and less motivated. But at least there wasn't the guilt. Just regret.

Investigators, lawyers, doctors, and nurses were his only visitors for weeks. Longjohn was in his own room, kept away from Mark so they couldn't coach each other on their stories until the case was closed.

They wouldn't tell him where Jennifer was.

After twenty days in the dark, he finally got his answers. After getting the stitches out of his thigh and shoulder, he got his first visit. JAG lawyer Lieutenant Junior Grade Nathan Daniels. Still in his first year, or he'd be an O-3.

No further charges against him, and original charges dismissed after payment of damages.

Mark held his hand up to stop the young man's rambling. "Hang on a second. What payment of damages?"

Daniels dug through his stapled files. Mark though it was funny that the modern military still depended on pen and paper so much. Daniels leaned back like he had trouble seeing the small print. "Right. It looks like initial damage estimates were assigned to the co-defendants."

"And who are they?"

"That is not information I can give, sir. But I can say since some of them are dead—"

"Which ones?"

Daniels organized his files with a fussy smile. "That is not information I can give."

Mark pinched the bridge of his nose. A headache loomed on the horizon. "You mean ... I am a co-defendant with the men that tried to kill us? And since they're dead, I owe their part of the damages?"

"Not exactly. And in any event, you don't owe anything. It was covered by a connected party."

"Let me get this straight. When somebody tried to kill me, and shit got fucked up, I have to pay for it even though I was the victim."

"Well, not all of it. Just for what you were judged to be liable."

"And how much was it?"

"That is not—"

Mark waved him off. "Information you can't give me, I got it."

Daniels grinned. "It was substantial."

"So now what?"

Daniels dug into his files again. "I have several forms for you to sign, and then you will be remanded to standard care until your discharge."

"That's it?"

"Isn't that enough?"'

Mark was taken aback by his sincerity. "What do you mean?"

Daniels set a stack of papers on Mark's good thigh. "You are alive after a terrible ordeal. According to your records, for the second time. No charges against you, and the best medical care in the world. What more do you want?"

"My boats back?"

"Sorry, but no. And your marina privileges have been revoked until further notice."

"Well, with no boat or place to live, what does it matter? But I get what you're saying."

"You'll get the houseboat back after the investigation concludes."

Daniels pulled a gold pen from his inside pocket. Clicked it opened and handed it over. Mark started signing. "When will that be?"

"Between four and twelve months."

"Jesus, why so long?"

Daniels retrieved his pen and jogged the signed papers back into his folder. "To be honest, the money required has already been paid, you have been cleared, and the *bad guys* are dead. There is no rush. But if it makes you feel better, you haven't heard from the city yet."

Mark didn't say goodbye when Daniels left.

Before Mark could think on what Daniels had told him, there was another knock on the door. It opened before he could tell whoever it was to go away, and a large bald man with a mean beard stepped in. Every lump and vein was visible through his tight polo shirt. "You Adler?" he asked. His rough voice sounded like an affectation to Mark.

"I am."

The man nodded. "It seems obvious, I guess, but I had to make sure."

"And you are?"

The man thrust his hand out and crossed over to the bed in a near jog. "Don St. James."

Mark could see it. The strength in Jennifer's jaw. The way she moved. The direct gaze. "Jennifer's father."

A stiff shake that bordered on painful before Don released his grip. "That's right. And I don't want to bother you, but I wanted to … thank you for taking care of my little girl."

Mark chuckled. "I didn't do much."

"That's not what she said."

"No, she took care of herself. I'd be dead without her."

"Really?" Don leaned back like he was surprised.

"Where is she?" Mark asked. "Is she okay?"

Don sighed. "I'm not sure." He held his hands up and shook his head. "That's not what I mean. She's fine, but she's not herself."

"What do you mean?"

Don sneered like thinking caused him pain. "She won't talk to us."

"Join the club." Mark looked away from Don's stare. It looked too much like judgement.

"She wants to be alone."

"I get it."

Don lowered his fingers to touch Mark's shoulder. "I don't think you do. I came to tell you she's going to leave. She asked me to tell you goodbye for her."

There was the regret. She was gone.

Mark nodded. "I guess *you're* the connected party that paid for the damages?"

Don's smile was oddly proud. "We had to sell a helicopter to cover it. There was a lot."

"Well, thanks. I don't deserve it, but I appreciate it."

"You might not, but she does."

"Yeah, she's great."

"And that brings me to one more thing," Don said.

"Don't bother. I won't come looking for her. No threats necessary."

Don slumped like he had lost his breath. Without another word, he turned and marched out. He left the door hanging open behind him.

"Asshole," Mark muttered.

He laid his head back and closed his eyes, but instead of falling asleep, he remembered how it felt when Jennifer was on his chest after they had both nearly died.

Chapter Thirty-Nine

THREE MONTHS LATER

Mark slid the cooler back behind the controls and stored the knives in the locked compartment next to it. He and Drake had been out again. Almost sixty-five fish between them.

His new boat was much smaller than the last one had been, but he had stopped taking people out for money. Now, it was just the people he most wanted to be around, although the one he most wanted to go out with hadn't come back yet.

Jennifer had left as soon as the investigation was over. No calls or messages. He understood. She had been through a lot. She probably needed time to process it all, or whatever.

He couldn't help thinking the reason she never came back was because of him.

Most days, he looked at all his new scars in the mirror and thought about how she had felt pressed up against him during the storm. It was better than thinking of the explosion on the *Northville*, though he hadn't had a nightmare about that damned boat since she left.

He would have told her that was proof she was a good person, but she was gone, so…

His new brace kept his knee from collapsing, but he was in for a replacement consultation in a couple of weeks. The VA took a while sometimes, but that was okay. He was getting by. He only drank now because he wanted to, and the minute he felt like he *needed* to, he put the lid back on the bottle and moved on. He hadn't been drunk since … he sighed to himself in frustration. Everything in his life was now measured by when it happened in relation to *her*. Before he met her, after she left. It was like he was mourning a divorce, and they hadn't even been married.

They hadn't been *anything*.

Longjohn told him the change Jennifer had made in him had been profound. When Mark had asked what it was, Longjohn just smiled. He was up in Michigan visiting some of his grandkids, but it would be getting cold up there soon, so Mark had that to look forward to. But not much else. Just the routine. Get up, work out, fish, drink, rinse, repeat.

He had put the boat on the trailer an hour ago. He took his time washing it off and putting things away. Really just keeping busy so he didn't have to go back to the RV. That's when he tended to think the most. Everything felt like a waste lately.

He climbed down the ladder to stand on the trawler's tongue so he could hop to the ground. He paused when he heard footsteps grinding on the gravel behind him. When he turned to see a woman in a tropical outfit under a matching straw hat, he caught his breath.

But it wasn't Jennifer.

It was Nancy Perlmutter.

She stood with the sun behind her, but he could see her smile below her oversized sunglasses. She held her arms out, and Mark stepped into her embrace.

"Hey, girl," he said.

She gave him a fierce squeeze before stepping back. "Hey, yourself."

"How have you been?"

She looked down at the ground. "As good as I can be. Harold passed."

Mark felt like an idiot. He should have known. "I'm so sorry. Is there anything you need?"

She laughed. "He said you would say that. He liked you."

"I liked *him*."

"We both did."

They stared at each other, and Mark wondered why she was there. She nodded once and pulled her purse around. "I'm here to pay you for the charter."

Mark held his hands up. "No, no. It was my pleasure."

She dug into her purse undeterred. "You know, he talked about it for a month and a half? Almost three times as long as the doctors had given him? You may not know it, and you may not believe it, but you had an impact on him. I bet you have it on most people."

"I don't know about that."

"Anyway, it doesn't matter. He wanted you to get paid, and you're not going to deny a dying man his last wish."

Mark lowered his head. "Okay."

"Good, because I have to get going, because as much as I like you and what you did, I can't stand to be reminded of him just yet. Maybe we'll cross paths down here someday."

Mark thought about how Jennifer had left, and he resisted the urge to say, "I doubt it."

She held out a thin envelope. Tears tracked out from under her dark lenses. Mark nodded as he took the envelope. "Thank you."

She laughed. "No, Mark. Thank *you*." She rose on her toes for another hug before grabbing his head between her hands and kissing him on the lips. Just like Harold had done when he had last seen him.

Without another word, she turned and walked away. Mark opened the envelope. His bad knee almost let loose. It was a check for twenty-five thousand dollars.

He raised it up in protest, but Nancy had already climbed up into her black SUV. When it pulled away, it revealed a Dodge Ram behind it.

Mark froze like he was hailing an invisible cab.

When Jennifer dropped out of the truck's cab, he stuffed the check back in the envelope and moved to greet her.

"Hey," he said.

She wore cutoff jean shorts and a white tank top. Her hair was a short spiky bob that made her look like a fairy who had been turned into a human. She smiled as she pointed at his boat. "You take people out on that thing?"

He looked back at it. "Yeah, sometimes."

"How much do you charge?"

He shrugged. "It depends on what you want."

She smiled and looked up at the sky. "You know, for a long time, I didn't *know* what I wanted. I always relied on other people to tell me. But somebody taught me something about myself."

"Oh yeah? What was that?"

She turned to look back at the truck, shielding her eyes against the setting sun. A faint scar ran up her leg through the tattoo. "He taught me that my choice is important. Not *more* important than any other, but *as* important. It was a weird thing to learn." She turned back around and met his gaze. "And for some reason, I resented you for it."

Mark wanted to apologize, but he remained silent.

"I sold my shares back to my parents. Left the company, left home. But no matter what, I couldn't stop thinking about that lesson. About you."

Mark couldn't stay quiet any longer. "I've thought about you every single day."

Her shy smile quivered at the edges before breaking into a sparkling grin. She pointed at his boat. "I've never really fished before. I'm not sure I'll like it."

"Well, I could take you out. Show you how it's done."

"Yeah, but will I have a good time?"

"As long as you keep an open mind."

She stepped forward and put her forehead on his chest. When he wrapped his arms around her, she settled into him, and he dropped his cheek onto the top of her head.

"Well, that's why I'm here," she said.

The End

About the Author

Sawyer Black writes dark and violent fiction for people who secretly love puppies and rainbows. In addition to being a U.S. Army veteran, he's also a beardsman. In fact, that's where all his ideas come from. The beard. Speculative stories about struggle and triumph and brutal emotion, written mostly for his ideal reader, his wife of nearly twenty-five years. He's an independent woman who likes cigars and margaritas, and he holds the deep belief that the earth is round.

Also By Sawyer Black

The Monstrous Series

Soulless

Monstrous Book One

Monstrous Book Two

Monstrous Book Three

Stand Alone Novels

Zoomers vs Boomers

Analog Heart

Born To Die